A Mermaid in Middle Grade

BOOK 2
THE FAR-FINDING RING

KNOWLEDGE FOREST
PRESS

A.M. LUZZADER

Copyright © 2020 by Amanda Luzzader

www.amandaluzzader.com

Published by Knowledge Forest Press
P.O. Box 6331
Logan, UT 84341

Ebook ISBN-13: 978-1-949078-13-8
Paperback ISBN-13: 978-1-949078-14-5
Hardback ISBN-13: 978-1-949078-15-2

Cover design by Sleepy Fox Studio

Developmental and Copy Editing by Chadd VanZanten and
Barbra Yardley

Proofreading by Tell Tale Editing

Interior illustrations by Chadd VanZanten

For Olivia Mae,
the cutest little mermaid

ACTIVITY KIT

Visit www.subscribepage.com/amandaluzzader to sign up to receive an occasional newsletter with information about promotions and new releases. From this site you'll also be able to download a **Free Activity Kit for A Mermaid in Middle Grade.**

CHAPTER ONE

*B*rynn couldn't believe her good luck. It was her first day of the second semester at Crystal Water Middle School, and not only did she have Windy Meyers as a teacher for magic class again, but this semester, her very best friend, Jade Sands, was in her class. Brynn and Jade had been besties since they were wee merbabies, since they were both in diapers, since before they even learned to swim.

On the first day of the new semester, Brynn and Jade arranged to sit on the front row of desks, right next to each other.

"This is going to be the best semester of middle school ever," said Brynn to Jade. "I already loved Mrs. Meyers and her class, but I hardly knew anyone in the class. This time, it's going to be better than ever."

"I know," squealed Jade. "I wonder if we could get our schedules changed and have all our classes together."

"Doubtful," replied Brynn, "but if I had to pick just one class for us to have together, it would definitely be this one. My favorite school subject, taught by my favorite teacher, sitting next to my favorite friend."

The mermaids heaved dreamy, best-friend sighs as they unpacked their notebooks and pens. Then, from a desk behind them, there came an exaggerated, sarcastic, mock best-friend sigh.

There sat William Beach, a merboy who had been in Brynn's magic class the previous semester. Jade and Brynn both knew Will, and although they'd had their ups and downs, they did not dislike the merboy. But now, Will folded his arms across his chest and put on a cocky, scornful expression.

"I guess you two besties are gonna sigh at each other and braid friendship bracelets all semester?" he asked with a dramatic eye-roll.

"Oh," exclaimed Jade excitedly, "friendship bracelets!"

"Yeah, great idea, Will!" said Brynn with a giggle. "Thanks!"

"Brynn, *dahling*, what color do you want?" Jade was using her "dramatic actor" voice.

"You decide, *dahling*—something to match my

eyes, perhaps?" said Brynn. "What color would you like?"

"Silver and gold for me, please, *dahling*!"

Will rolled his eyes again, but the girls laughed and paid him no attention.

The bell rang, and Mrs. Windy Meyers swam to the front of the class. She was a kind and thoughtful teacher with yellow hair. She had helped Brynn at the first of the year when she was struggling with magic. Windy was exactly what Brynn wanted to be like when she was older—smart, polished, talented at magic, and very helpful. Brynn had a tendency to daydream during her other classes, but she tried not to when in Mrs. Meyers' class. Magic was too interesting for that.

Brynn and Jade sat attentively in their chairs, their hands folded on their desks.

"I'm glad to see so many of my students back from the first semester," said Windy.

Brynn thought that maybe Windy had looked directly at her when she said this, but she couldn't be sure.

Because it was the first day of the new semester, Mrs. Meyers went over the class rules and the spells the class would cover that semester. Jade and Brynn raised their hands and answered Mrs. Meyers' questions.

"We touched briefly last semester on magic amplifiers—the various methods you can utilize to strengthen a spell. We'll be covering those in much more detail this time around."

Upon hearing this, Jade and Brynn sat up even straighter, though this was hardly possible.

Mrs. Meyers continued. "We will learn how to perfect the amplifiers, especially the friendship amplifier and also the singing amplifier. Be prepared to partner up with a friend to practice that amplifier. You'll be doing a lot of partner work this term."

Brynn and Jade side-glanced at each other, then they grinned and nodded. William Beach scoffed.

"And if you don't already happen to have a friend in the class," said Windy, "this might be a good chance to make a new friend."

Jade and I don't have to worry about that, Brynn thought.

The rest of the class passed quickly, and soon the bell rang. There was a commotion in the classroom as the students gathered their things and chattered with each other. Most of the students in the room were talking and seahorsing around with a friend or even several friends, but Brynn noticed out of the corner of her eye that William Beach was on his own, not interacting with any other students. No one gave him a playful shove or said, "See you at lunch!" He spoke to no one and no one spoke to him. Brynn remembered that Jade had once said that Will didn't have many friends. At that moment, it looked like maybe he didn't have any. She wondered if that were true, and she wondered why.

"So, if friendship is a mer-magic amplifier," mused Jade, "do you think best-friendship is even better?"

"Oh, totally," replied Brynn, forgetting about Will for the moment. "This is going to be so fun. We're going to make the best partners."

"You know, we really should make some friendship bracelets," said Jade. "Maybe that will help our mer-magic, too."

"Yes, *dahling*!" replied Brynn.

"Oh, brother," muttered Will as he moped out of the classroom.

Brynn wasn't joking around about best-friendship and mer-magic. She really did hope it would help. She'd been Jade's best friend for longer than either of them could remember, and Jade's family had always lived just a quick swim from Brynn's house. The friends were born only a day apart, so the mermaids had been in the hospital together, in the nursery together, and getting together for playdates since almost before either of them knew what it meant to have a friend or be a friend. Their parents had pictures of them together when they were merbabies, holding hands, with matching shell-shaped pacifiers in their little mer-mouths.

Brynn's next class was math with Mrs. Shelley

Smith, but Jade had to go to singing class next, so they each went to their different classes.

"Until we meet again, *dahling*," said Jade in her dramatic-actor voice.

The two mermaids blew each other lingering, dramatic-actor kisses as they went their separate ways, then broke out in giggles as they receded from sight.

Brynn found her math class, looked around the room, and took the only seat still unoccupied. As she unpacked her textbook and pencil, she was a little startled to see Will in the desk beside her. He grinned a smirky grin at her.

"You again?" groaned Brynn as she slumped into the seat.

"Hey, I was here first," Will protested. "It's beginning to seem like you're following me so you can sit next to me in every class." He chuckled.

"Not likely," said Brynn.

Not long before, Will had let Brynn off the hook for the bet they made when Brynn used the magic talisman of Lostland to pass her magic class midterm. At the time, Brynn thought it was very mature and kind of Will to do so. She wasn't sure how things had become unfriendly between her and Will, but somehow it had—and it had happened so fast, too. Brynn didn't know it, but just a few unkind words or a little bit of thoughtlessness could sink a friendship before it ever set sail.

"At least when I have a class with Jade," added Brynn in a sassy tone, "I don't have to put up with your annoying sarcasm all by myself."

"What's with you and Jade, anyway?" asked Will.

"What about us?" returned Brynn with a glare.

"You're only friends with each other and not anyone else."

"That's not true," said Brynn, now with a slightly superior tone in her voice. "We have other friends. But we are what you call *best friends*. Perhaps the concept is foreign to you, William Beach."

For what seemed to be the one-hundredth time since the school day began, Will rolled his eyes.

"Allow me to explain," sassed Brynn. "You can have an unlimited number of friends, but you can only have one *best* friend, and your best friend's best friend is always you."

"She's only your best friend because you've known each other for so long and grew up close to each other. Best friends are just a fake idea that people make up so they don't have to be nice to anyone else."

"Actually, Will," said Brynn, examining the scales on her tailfin as though the conversation had started to bore her, "Jade is my best friend because she is kind and smart and funny, and we like all the same things, and we understand each other. And she helped me rescue my pet turtle one time. She'd do anything for me, and I'd do anything for her."

Will began to roll his eyes once again, but then decided against it because it would take too much effort.

"You're just jealous," Brynn continued, turning herself to face the front of the class, "because you don't *have* a best friend, and even if you did have a best friend, they wouldn't be as awesome as *my* best friend." Here again, Brynn wasn't certain how things had gotten so cold and spiteful with Will. What had happened?

Then she thought, *He started it, that's what happened.*

Will didn't say anything in response to Brynn. What could he say? He just scowled, as he often did, and then he also turned in his seat to face the front of the classroom. Brynn looked at him for a moment longer and was sure she detected a hint of hurt in Will's expression. Had she gone too far? Or did he deserve it? She wasn't sure who Will's friends were, or if he even had one.

When Mrs. Meyers had announced they'd be choosing partners in class to experiment with the mer-magical concept of friendship amplification, it had seemed like such a fun prospect, but then she'd noticed that Will had no one in the class to high-five or wink at. Brynn wondered if the announcement might be sad news for someone like Will, who didn't have a friend in the class. What if he didn't have a single friend in the whole school? Was that why Will was so snarky and sarcastic to Jade and Brynn?

If it were, Brynn decided, there wasn't anything she could do about it. She and Jade were the best of friends. It couldn't be helped.

Instead of being jealous of someone else's friendship, Brynn thought, *Will should work on making his own friends.*

CHAPTER TWO

*A*fter dinner that evening, Brynn's parents, Dana and Adrian, were watching the Night-Sea News on the shell-a-vision. Brynn lay sprawled on the living room floor with her paper, pens, and markers, drawing different designs of friendship bracelets that she and Jade might create for each other. She couldn't simply make a friendship bracelet—she had to develop concepts and various ideas. Then she'd compare them, consult with Jade, and only then would she actually start making a bracelet. And so there was a narrow bracelet of delicate strands of moss with dangly seashells. There was another one with thick strands of seagrass with little beads made of agate and sea glass.

As she worked, Brynn paid no attention to the news—it was always "*government this*" and "*economy that*"—but then she heard a reporter say, "Sawfield Selkie Sisters."

Her head snapped up, and she fixed her big blue eyes on the shell-a-vision.

The Night-Sea News reporter said, "Scarlet and Sapphire, the Sawfield Selkie Sisters, were apprehended today just outside the city of Great Reef. The sisters in crime had previously been convicted of luring human ships into dangerous waters, but they recently escaped from their prison cell at an undisclosed location and have been at large for more than a month. They've been accused of having tried their nefarious crimes again."

"I think I can say for sure that they're guilty," mumbled Brynn to herself.

During the previous semester, Brynn had unintentionally assisted Phaedra, the sea witch, in releasing Sapphire and Scarlet Sawfield from their underground prison cell. She gritted her teeth nervously as she gazed at the shell-a-vision screen. There, she saw the Sawfield Selkie Sisters as they were led, handcuffed, into a big government building. Mer-police officers swam alongside each of them, and the selkies themselves wore their wicked, mischievous grins as though they might try to escape again at any moment.

Brynn sat up on the floor. She noticed her parents were also watching closely. The three of them exchanged nervous glances.

"After their escape," the reporter continued, "the infamous sisters and a sea witch, who goes by the name of Phaedra, attempted to sink a human ship at Sunshine Lagoon, but were stopped by mer-authorities and a group of local residents. The criminals evaded capture at the time, but mer-police have been on the lookout for them ever since. Meanwhile, there have been reports of at least three additional attempts to sink oceangoing vessels of the humans, and the involvement of Phaedra, the sea witch, is suspected."

It was of course Brynn, her parents, and her best friend, Jade, who had stopped the selkies and Phaedra from sinking the ship that day at Sunshine Lagoon. It bothered Brynn a little that the reporter didn't bother to mention that.

The reporter went on. "Now that they have been captured, the selkies will be returning to jail, this time in a more secure location. The sea witch, Phaedra, is still on the loose. Mer-authorities are asking anyone with information on the whereabouts of Phaedra to contact them through the appropriate dolphin channels."

Brynn's mother, Dana, turned off the shell-a-vision. Brynn felt goosebumps form on her arms.

"The sea witch wants to get revenge on me," said Brynn. "I'm worried she'll do a spell on me or something."

Adrian and Dana looked at each other.

"Sweetie," said Dana. "I want you to know that your dad and I will do everything we can to keep you safe. And the mer-police are working hard to find and capture the sea witch, so I don't think you have anything to worry about. Just in case, though, you should probably stick close to home for a while."

"What about Tully?" Brynn asked.

Tully was Brynn's beloved pet sea turtle, and while sea turtles could stay underwater for a long time, they had to surface a couple of times each day to get fresh breaths of air.

"I'll take him for his surface walks for a while," said Adrian with a smile. "Just until they capture Phaedra."

Brynn frowned. She didn't like the idea of staying at home so much. She liked taking Tully on walks, or riding the speed-current to the kelpshake shop, and she loved going to the kelp forest (which was her favorite place in the whole wide ocean) with her best friend, Jade.

Nevertheless, Brynn understood why she needed to keep a low profile. Phaedra was unpredictable and dangerous, and she frightened Brynn more than a little bit. Brynn had actually helped Phaedra with her wicked plan to retaliate against the humans, but in the end, she'd fouled up Phaedra's schemes, and the sea witch was not happy about that. Just before the sea witch had escaped, she had pointed her long, white finger at Brynn and hissed, "You'll pay for this."

Brynn didn't know exactly what she meant by that, but it couldn't be anything good. It was widely rumored that sea witches could turn merfolk into sea slugs, and Brynn had spent many an unpleasant moment wondering what it would be like if that's what Phaedra decided to do to her.

"What if she turns me into a slug?" Brynn blurted.

"A slug?" asked Adrian.

"Yeah, I heard she's done that before."

"Nobody is going to turn you into a slug," said Dana. "Now, don't worry. We're going to get this taken care of, and for now, we'll just be a little extra cautious. Not because we think anything might happen, but just because it doesn't hurt to play things on the safe side."

"Yeah, besides," added Brynn's father, "if she did turn you into a sea slug, you would be the cutest sea slug of all. We'd be so proud."

"Dad!" Brynn protested. She knew that Adrian was trying to make her feel better by making a joke, but Brynn wasn't reassured.

When Brynn went to bed that night, she could hear her parents talking. She swam up out of bed and pressed her ear against the door. Tully followed behind her.

"Something needs to be done," said Dana. "She really did make a threat against Brynn."

"I know," said Adrian. "But the mer-authorities are working on it. We just need to give them time."

"It's been nearly two months," said Dana. "What if she shows up here, in Fulgent? What if she does try to do something to Brynn?"

"I'll talk to the mer-police tomorrow and see if they have any leads," said Adrian.

"And what if they don't?" asked Dana.

Her father sighed. "We're just going to hope she can be found. She can't stay in hiding forever."

Brynn swam back to her bed and fiddled with her hair. Her parents sounded worried, and if they were worried, that made Brynn really worried. She didn't like seeing them this way.

"Tully," she whispered. "I'm glad you're here because you'll protect me, right?"

Tully seemed to nod his head, but then again, that's what he almost always did when Brynn asked him a question.

"We'll protect each other," said Brynn. "I just need to learn some more magic, then things will be better. I still can't conjure a bubble of protection spell; I need to learn that. And then maybe I can learn some spell reversals."

Brynn remembered how her mother, Dana, had used a spell reversal on the sea witch when they tried to stop Phaedra from sinking the humans' boat. Her mother had been able to redirect Phaedra's spells right back at her.

"Ooo, and I need to learn to shoot magical missiles and bombs."

Brynn imagined the sea witch casting a spell at her to turn her into a sea slug. She pictured herself holding her hands up and bouncing the spell back at her like it was a mirror, and then the sea witch transformed into a blubbery gray slug.

But then Brynn sighed.

"Thank goodness Jade's going to be my partner in magic class. I'm going to need the power of friendship if I'm going to be able to summon those powerful spells."

Tully snuggled up to Brynn's tailfin. Brynn began to feel better as she thought about going to magic class with Jade for the next semester, and Brynn was smiling when she finally fell asleep.

CHAPTER THREE

*W*hile the sea witch was on the loose, Brynn's parents discouraged her from playing outside for too long or straying too far from home, but they didn't have any problem if Brynn played at Jade's house. And so when the weekend arrived, that was exactly where Brynn went.

The two mermaids made friendship bracelets, ate cookies, and then tried out different hairstyles. Brynn braided Jade's long white hair, and then Jade twisted Brynn's lavender locks into elaborate curls on top of her head.

They listened to songs by their favorite mer-music band, Jay Barracuda and the Killer Whales, while they flipped through *Tigershark Beat* and the glossy and glamorous pages of *Young Mermaids* magazine. They *ooo*ed and *aww*ed in unison at the mermodels with their glittery tailfins and luscious flowing hair and dazzling makeup.

"Isn't Jay Barracuda dreamy?" Jade said as the music played.

Somewhere, somewhere, inside the ocean, ocean

A sweet, sweet mermaid has stolen my heart!

Jade sang along with the music.

So swim to me again! Just like you did last summer.

Swim to me again! You have my heart!

"I love this song," said Jade. She turned and smiled at Brynn. "In fact, I love singing. I want to be one of the Singing Starfish when I grow up."

"You will be, Jade. You are learning so much at your singing lessons, and even without the lessons, I've always thought you have one of the best voices," said Brynn. She really did think Jade was an incredible singer.

A little while later, they played with their Mermies, which were small, poseable mermaid and mermen dolls with clothing and accessories like sunglasses and hats shellphones. They combed the Mermies' hair and assembled coordinating outfits. Jade pretended that her Mermie doll, the one with the white hair, was a famous pop star. Brynn pretended that her Mermie, the one with lavender hair, was the most talented mergician in all the ocean. She was asked to protect all the merfolk before going on a date with a hunky, blue-haired Mermie merman who wanted to be a stay-at-home dad.

After playing Mermies, the two mermaids lounged on Jade's bed, staring at the ceiling lit with magical rocks.

"Are you bored?" asked Jade. "I'm bored."

"I'm deathly bored," said Brynn. "I wish we could go outside to the kelp forest."

"Me, too," said Jade wistfully.

Brynn turned onto her side to look at Jade. "I'm just glad we are in magic class together. It's going to be so much fun."

"It was meant to be, Brynn!"

"Yeah."

The mermaids were quiet for a few moments. Then Jade looked over at Brynn with a mischievous look in her eye and a smile on her face. She playfully slapped Brynn with her tailfin.

"Tag!" she yelled. "You're it!"

Jade darted out her bedroom door, leaving a crazy trail of bubbles behind her. Brynn squealed and chased her down the hallway.

The craggy cave homes of merfolk were never overly large, so Jade didn't have many places to run or hide. She dashed out of her room, swam in a circle for someplace to escape to, and then dove directly into her parents' bedroom. Brynn was a mere kick of the tailfin behind Jade. When Jade went around one side of her parents' bed, Brynn cornered her.

"Gotcha!" shouted Brynn.

Jade gave a giggling shout and tried to dive past,

but Brynn tackled her, and the two mermaids swirled together in a tangle of laughing and wrestling and tickling.

Just before they left the room, laughing and panting with exhaustion, Brynn spotted an interesting little box on a dresser in a corner of the room. It was a small, ornate jewelry box, fashioned from bright coral and abalone shell. It gleamed beautifully in the afternoon light, and its lid was open slightly.

As Brynn passed by it, she noticed that the box was evidently crafted to hold only one article of jewelry: a magnificent string of pearls. For some reason, it caught Brynn's eye, and she couldn't stop staring at it. The necklace had ten pearls, and for Brynn it was absolutely captivating to see. It seemed to glow with a glimmer of its own. She paused and then swam closer to get a better look.

"Is this your mother's necklace?" Brynn asked, her voice soft with wonder.

"Yeah," replied Jade, joining Brynn at the dresser. Even Jade's eyes got a little wider as she gazed at the pearls. "Isn't it gorgeous? Mom wore it on her wedding day. It was a gift she was given for the work she did as a doctor at the Merfolk General Hospital."

"It's lovely," sighed Brynn.

"Yep. And guess what?" said Jade. "It's enchanted as well."

"Really?"

Jade nodded. "It can strengthen spells by ten times."

"Wowee!" said Brynn, not taking her eyes from the pearls.

"But nowadays my mom only wears it for special occasions."

"Imagine if we had necklaces like that," Brynn mused. "It'd be so awesome. Just picture us in magic class—looking gorgeous and powerful and casting spells multiplied by ten times!"

"It was a big deal when the hospital gave it to her. The pearls came from different areas of the ocean. It was on the news and everything. It's the only one like it in the entire world."

"That's amazing," whispered Brynn. "Do you think I could try it on?"

"Oh, no," said Jade. "Sorry, but my mom is very protective of it. She doesn't even let me wear it. In fact, I don't think she'd like us touching it."

Brynn frowned. She had no intention of going against the wishes of Jade's mom, but she sure would have loved to try on the pearls.

"Hey," said Jade. "Let's go back to my room and paint our nails."

"Good idea," said Brynn, but her gaze lingered on the pearls as they swam from the room.

Back in Jade's room, Brynn picked a glittery pink nail polish, and Jade chose a turquoise color. Jade always painted her nails very slowly and carefully, with her brow furrowed and her tongue sticking out of the corner of her mouth. Brynn just didn't have that much patience. And Brynn's nails never looked as tidy as Jade's, but at least she was finished much faster. By the time Brynn's nails were dry, Jade still had six more fingers to paint.

She waited for a while for Jade to catch up, but then she said, "I'm going to grab a drink."

"Okay," said Jade without looking up from her nails.

As Brynn swam to the kitchen, she passed by Jade's parents' bedroom and spotted the jewelry box again. There was something that was so enticing about the necklace. Brynn felt as though the string of pearls was practically calling her name, and she knew she must have another look at them. She glanced back down the hallway, but Jade was still busy with her nails. Jade's mom and dad were both still at work at the hospital.

Brynn decided just to dart in for a quick peek.

But when she was in front of it again, the necklace seemed to call to her, telling her to wear it. Brynn wondered if that was part of the enchantment. She lifted the necklace out of the box and tilted her head to examine it from every angle. It was positively glorious. Each pearl was perfectly spherical, smooth, and lustrous. Each pearl caught the light and reflected it like starlight through sea mist.

"Wowee!" Brynn whispered again.

Mrs. Sands must have done some really important work to have been given such a wonderful gift. As a doctor, Mrs. Sands helped merpeople to get well every day from illnesses and injuries that mermagical spells couldn't heal. Brynn hoped that one day, she could also do something that important and have a beautiful necklace to show for it.

Wisely, Brynn didn't put the string of pearls around her neck. As much as she wanted to, she didn't. Instead, Brynn sighed, admired the pearls for a few seconds more, and put the necklace back in the box.

The necklace made Brynn think of the talisman from Lostland she had used to cheat on her magic midterm exam. The talisman necklace used a kind of magic that caused her to be mean to a lot of people, and Brynn had concluded it was definitely not worth it. But Brynn had to admit that she liked how the Lostland talisman had increased her ability to summon and cast mer-magical spells. Because the string of pearls had been a gift from the Merfolk General Hospital, Brynn knew it could only have been enchanted with the best of mer-magic. She wondered what it would be like to be able to increase her magical powers, but not have such awful side effects. Besides, the strand of pearls was probably even more powerful than the talisman of Lostland. If the talisman could have increased spells by ten times, there was no way that Ian Fletcher would have given it away—not for ten full-grown work turtles. He would have kept it for himself or given it to Phaedra.

"Brynn?" Jade called from her bedroom. "Where are you? I thought you were just getting a drink."

Brynn startled as if she had been shaken from a trance.

"I'm coming," she replied. Then she gave the string of pearls a last longing look and swam back to Jade's bedroom.

he next day, while Brynn was in her bedroom, she heard a loud knock on their cave door. She stayed in her bedroom, but listened to see if she could figure out who it was.

"Hi, Samantha," said Dana. "How are you? Come in, come in."

It was Samantha Sands, Jade's mom.

"Can I get you something?" said Brynn's mom.

"Hi, Dana," said Jade's mom. "No, nothing for me, thank you."

For some reason, Jade's mom didn't sound happy. Then there came a few moments of quiet. Brynn cocked her head to listen more closely, thinking maybe they were talking too quietly for her to hear, but then Brynn's mom spoke again.

"Is everything okay, Samantha?" said Dana. "Is something wrong?"

"Dana, I don't know how to tell you this. I have some, well, some unpleasant business to ask you about," said Samantha. "We need to have a talk with Brynn."

A chill swam straight down Brynn's back and into her scales and on to the tips of her tailfin. What had she done this time? She thought about this for a moment before she realized she hadn't done anything. For some reason, however, this wasn't a relief.

Brynn heard her mother invite Samantha into the front room. Brynn drifted quietly to her bedroom door and cracked it open so that she could hear better.

Jade's mother continued. "Our family went out together yesterday evening, and when we got back, I discovered that my cherished string of pearls was missing. You know the one? The string of ten pearls?"

"Of course," said Dana breathlessly. "It's an amazing piece of jewelry! It was a gift for your work at the hospital, wasn't it?"

"Yes, that's the one," answered Samantha in a shaky tone. "It's very precious to me." She paused for a long time, and then continue as though she almost could not form the words. "It's very precious, and it's *missing*."

Brynn felt a chill run from the top of her head to the tip of her tail.

"Oh, no," said Dana. "You must be worried sick. But—what's this got to do with Brynn?"

Yeah, thought Brynn. *What's this got to do with me?*

There was another quiet moment. Brynn thought maybe Jade's mother was fighting back tears.

"Well, Jade swears she didn't touch it," Samantha continued after another few seconds, "but she mentioned that Brynn had seen it and acted very interested in it. We think Brynn may have, well, we think she may have taken it."

Some very odd things happened to Brynn when she heard Jade's mother say this. Her cheeks got warm. Tiny tears sprang into her eyes. She wanted to hide under her bed. All of these things happened to Brynn even though she knew she hadn't taken the string of pearls. She felt guilty even though she'd done nothing wrong.

"Could there be some kind of misunderstanding?" asked Brynn's mother. Her voice was quiet but confused. "I just can't imagine Brynn would do anything like that."

"Well, maybe she wanted to admire them more," said Samantha. "Maybe she thought she could borrow them because she's a family friend. Could I talk to Brynn? Perhaps it is a misunderstanding, and Brynn could clear things up. We've looked all over the house and even used mer-magic to search for it."

Dana called for Brynn and asked her to join come into the front room.

Despite the embarrassment Brynn was feeling, she was actually quite eager to tell Samantha she hadn't taken the pearls. She turned to Tully, who lay on the bed dozing.

"Wish me luck, Tully," she said.

Tully raised his head, but it was obvious he had no idea what was happening.

Then Brynn swallowed hard and took a deep breath before swimming out into the front room. It was very curious, this feeling of guilt about something she hadn't done. She knew very well she would never simply steal something from her best friend's mother, and yet she felt very afraid.

"Sweetie," said Dana as Brynn came floating into the room, "Mrs. Sands' string of pearls has gone missing. Do you know anything about that?"

Brynn shook her head.

"But you saw it, didn't you?" asked Samantha.

"Well, yes, I saw it," Brynn admitted, "while I was at your house playing with Jade. At the sleepover. It's very beautiful. The pearls, I mean. But I didn't take it."

"Are you sure?" asked Samantha. Her voice was beginning to sound angry. "You didn't even touch it?"

Brynn swallowed again. "I might have touched it," she confessed hastily, her voice quavering. "Just for a second. But I put it back in the jewelry box. Honest!"

"Did you drop it? Is that what happened?" asked Mrs. Sands. "Did you take it somewhere else in the house?"

"No, I put it right back in the box," Brynn insisted. "It was there when I left."

"Brynn, please tell the truth," said Mrs. Sands. "This is very important."

Dana was looking back and forth between Samantha and Jade as though watching a game of ping-pong.

"I'm not lying," Brynn insisted. "I picked it up just to look at it, but then I put it back in the box. I promise."

"It's okay that you touched it," said Mrs. Sands. "It's very beautiful. I understand. But that necklace means a lot to me. I need it back, Brynn. I need you to give it back to me."

"But I don't have it!" Brynn cried.

Dana held up a hand. "Brynn said she didn't take it, Samantha. I think we should believe her. Isn't it more likely that you've misplaced it yourself? Or someone else did? Perhaps it was stolen. Could it have fallen out of the box?"

"I already told you," said Samantha, and now she was genuinely angry. "We have looked everywhere. It simply is not in our house. I am sure of it. Someone had to have taken it, and the only other person who was in the house was Brynn. She's even confessed that she touched it."

The hot, stinging tears that had been threatening to fall from Brynn's eyes now came bursting out. "I put it back. I swear!"

"How about this," said Samantha testily. "Maybe, just maybe, you took it with you when you left our house, and you lost it on the way. Could that be it? Just tell me what happened so we'll know where to keep looking. Please don't lie, Brynn. I must have my pearls!"

"I think that's enough," said Dana. Her face was lined with worry and sadness. "I believe Brynn. If she says she didn't take the pearls, then she didn't take them."

Mrs. Sands laughed. "Wow. She's really got you wrapped around her finger, doesn't she? Lying is bad enough, Dana, but we're talking about stealing something very valuable. That necklace is irreplaceable. It's the only kind like it in the entire world, and it has a lot of sentimental value, too. I wore it when I married Jade's father. Plus, it's very powerful. It has a special enchantment that was created in a spell by all my co-workers at the hospital. The circumstances for its creation took years to arrange. If that necklace fell into the wrong hands, it could do a lot of damage."

"I can see how this must be very upsetting, Samantha," said Dana, "but I'm sure the pearls will turn up."

Samantha let out a heavy sigh. "I'm sorry to have to do this, Dana, but if Brynn won't confess to what she's done, I can't have her in my house, and she can't be friends with my Jade anymore."

Brynn's chin nearly hit the seafloor.

"Oh, Samantha," said Dana, "don't do that. Brynn and Jade have been best friends practically since they were born. Don't you think you might be jumping to conclusions? Don't you think this might be hasty? There's no proof that Brynn took anything."

"I have plenty of conclusions," snapped Samantha, "and I don't need to jump to any of them. We all know Brynn cheated on her magic class midterm, and as if that wasn't bad enough, she got Jade wrapped up in that trouble with the sea witch. Surely, you can see why I know it was her. And now, not just lying more, but stealing something of such great value? She's a bad influence, and I can see that it is rubbing off on Jade."

Brynn's heart was booming, and she looked back and forth between her mother and Jade's mother. Seeing that Samantha thought so poorly of her made Brynn feel awful. She wanted to go bury herself in the sand outside and hide forever.

"Just because Brynn looked at your pearls, that doesn't make her a suspect. And neither does the fact that she made mistakes in the past. Everyone makes mistakes. Brynn learned her lesson last semester and has already faced her consequences. As far as I'm concerned, that never needs to be mentioned again. She's been a good friend to Jade, and she's not a bad influence. They've been friends for so long. I think that would be really unfair to both mermaids."

Mrs. Sands shook her head. "Dana, she's fooling you. You need to give her some more discipline until she starts behaving. But, meanwhile, I have to do what's right for my daughter, and that means making sure she has high-quality friends who won't lead her down the wrong current." She turned to look at Brynn. "You stay away from Jade. Don't come to our house. Don't ride the speed-current with her. Don't even talk to her at school. You understand? I'll be telling Jade this as well, and there will be serious consequences for her if she disobeys me."

"Samantha, don't you think it might be good to think this over before you do something so drastic? Let's pause, sleep on it, and then talk more tomorrow," said Dana.

"Absolutely not!" said Samantha.

"But—" Brynn tried to say.

"I don't want to hear another word!" said Mrs. Sands. "When you're ready to return my necklace, we can talk then. But until that happens, Brynn Finley will have nothing to do with the Sands family." She swam to the door.

Dana placed a hand on Brynn's shoulder. Brynn looked up at her mother. Dana gave her a reassuring look, and Brynn kept quiet.

"Mrs. Sands, wait," said Dana. "Let's talk about this calmly."

"There are plenty of other mermaids who don't lie, cheat, or steal that my Jade can make friends with," said Mrs. Sands, who then angrily flicked her tail, and with a *harrumph!* she dove out the door and swam away.

"Mom!" cried Brynn. "I didn't take it! I swear!"

"I know, sweetie," said Dana. "I believe you."

"But she's not going to let me be around Jade anymore."

"Let's just give her some time," said Dana. "She was really angry just now. Sometimes anger can cloud people's judgment. It makes it so they can't think clearly. That necklace obviously means a lot to her, and I'm afraid she's taking it out on you. Let's let her think about it, and then maybe she'll come to her senses. Besides, that necklace is bound to turn up sooner or later."

Brynn hoped her mother was right. To have been called a liar, a thief, and a cheat made Brynn feel awful. It probably would have hurt less if she'd been punched in the stomach. To have someone who had known Brynn her whole life say such horrible things made her feel so ashamed and embarrassed. She wasn't sure what she was most upset about—not getting to see Jade or the fact that someone believed such awful things about her.

Dana, Adrian, and Tully all tried to cheer Brynn up.

"Hey! I got a great idea!" said Adrian later that evening. "Let's go out for clamburgers!"

Brynn shook her head. "Clamburgers are Jade's favorite," she said gloomily.

"Oh, I know!" said Dana. "Let's go for a walk in the kelp forest!"

Brynn shook her head again. "That's where Jade and I always hung out," she groaned.

Apparently, there wasn't anything they could do to remove the heavy weight that seemed to have been placed on Brynn's shoulders. Brynn could only think of one person she wanted to talk to about it, and that was Jade—the only merperson she wanted to talk to in the whole wide ocean was one she wasn't allowed to speak to.

CHAPTER FIVE

The weekend seemed to drag on for an eternity. Brynn kept hoping Mrs. Sands would change her mind or the necklace would be found or Jade would show up to explain that it had all been a big mix-up. She waited and waited. Brynn didn't really care how it was resolved; she just wanted *something* to happen so she could know she wasn't losing her best friend.

And so she was relieved when she saw Jade on Monday morning, apparently waiting for Brynn at the speed-current stop like she always did. Perhaps everything had been resolved.

"Jade!" cried Brynn, hurrying to the stop. "Hi!" She smiled broadly and swam right up to Jade.

But Jade wasn't smiling, and she shifted uncomfortably, looking around the speed-current stop as if to check if someone were watching them.

"Oh, Brynn," whimpered Jade. "It's just so awful. My mother is furious. She says I can't play with you or talk with you or even see you! I shouldn't even be talking to you now, but I guess I have to explain everything."

"I didn't take her necklace," said Brynn.

"I know you didn't," said Jade. "Of course, you wouldn't."

"That's a relief," said Brynn with a long, sad sigh. "It's good to know that my best friend doesn't think of me as a thief. That doesn't help the situation, though."

"No, it doesn't help at all. My mom is convinced. And it is very strange," said Jade. "We can't find the pearls anywhere. We've all looked and looked. It's disappeared! I spent the whole weekend looking for it, and I was even looking this morning before school. My mom is so sad about it. I'm going to keep searching for it until it's found."

"I don't understand," said Brynn, her brow furrowing. "Where could it have gone?"

Jade just shook her head sadly. "We went out to dinner, and when we got back, Mom went in her room, and that's when she noticed it was missing. The last time I saw it was when we were playing tag. She made me repeat to her everything we did, and I told her we looked at the necklace. I'm so sorry, Brynn."

"Jade, I did go and look at it again when you

were painting your nails, but I honestly didn't take it. I have no idea where it could be. Believe me, if I did, I would say so."

"I know, I know," said Jade. "But my mom is convinced you took it."

"So—what does this mean?" Brynn asked cautiously. "I can't hang out with you after school? We can't hang out or go places together?"

"No," said Jade. "My mom has forbidden me to have any contact with you."

"That's terrible."

"It gets worse," said Jade. "My mom called all my teachers. She doesn't want me eating lunch with you or even sitting by you. We can't do schoolwork together. Nothing! She's said that if she catches me hanging out with you, she'll make me quit my singing lessons and the choir, too."

"She can't do that," said Brynn. "You've always dreamed of being a singer. You need those lessons to keep improving. Plus, you love going to singing lessons!"

"I know," said Jade. "I guess that's why she told me that—she knows I'll have to do what she says and stay away from you."

"I would never want you to quit your voice training," said Brynn. Her heart began pounding, and she felt like she was being ripped in two. Brynn really did not want Jade to have to quit her singing lessons, but she also really didn't want to not see or talk with Jade.

Then, Brynn thought of something and gasped. "What about magic class? We were going to be partners. We have to do the friendship amplifiers."

Jade shook her head. "I'm sorry, I can't. My mom spoke with Mrs. Meyers already and told her not to let us be partners. She's talked to all my teachers."

"But you're my best friend!" cried Brynn.

"And you're mine!" replied Jade.

"What are we going to do?" Brynn asked.

"I don't know," said Jade. "I don't know if there's anything we can do. But I better go now. Sorry, Brynn. I don't want her to catch me talking to you. That would just make things worse. I'm so sorry!"

Jade swam onto the speed-current and was pulled away by the swift-moving water. She gave Brynn a melancholy goodbye wave as she retreated into the blue gloom of the sea. Brynn waved back and stood by herself at the speed-current stop.

A flurry of worries swirled around in Brynn's brain. Who would she sit with at lunch? Who would be her partner in magic class? What would she do on the weekends? Who would sing Jay Barracuda and the Killer Whales songs with her? What would she do without her best friend who'd been in her life since she was a merbaby?

Brynn found herself breathing hard and feeling unwell. The semester had started out so brilliantly.

Now, Brynn didn't even want to go to school, or do any mer-magic, or anything else. She couldn't imagine a life without Jade. However, there wasn't much else she could do, so Brynn sniffed, hiked her backpack up onto her shoulders, and swam onto the speed-current. In a sort of numb daze, she found a seat among the other riders.

The person sitting next to her elbowed her and said, "Hey, where's your twin?"

It was William Beach. Brynn wondered why he always seemed to show up at the worst moments.

"What? What did you say?" said Brynn, blinking her eyes as though she'd been shaken awake from a restless nap.

"Where's your twin, Jade?" asked Will. "Don't you two always ride the current together? Don't you do everything together? Aren't you two always joined at the hip?"

Technically, thought Brynn, *we* used *to do every-thing together. We* used *to be joined at the hip.* Brynn's chin quivered. *Don't cry,* she insisted, but her eyes seemed to ignore the demand, and her eyes welled with tears.

"Um, are you okay?" Will asked.

Don't cry, Brynn repeated in her mind.

"Is Jade sick or something?" he asked, then, with his usual snarky attitude, he added, "Or is she just sick of you?"

If Brynn had been in a better state of mind, she

might have laughed off Will's wisecrack, especially if she had Jade to back her up—having a friend always makes it easier to take it when someone is teasing you. But this time, she could not hold back her tears, and she began crying loudly.

"Her—mom—won't let Jade—see me—anymore," Brynn blubbered between sobs. "We're not best friends anymore." Brynn was embarrassed to have broken down in front of Will and the many speed-current passengers, but she couldn't help it.

Will rubbed his face, looking confused and embarrassed. He looked around at the other speed-current riders as though one of them might come to his aid, but none of them did. He chewed on his bottom lip and shifted around.

"I, uh, don't understand," said Will.

"The pearls!" Brynn blurted with a sob. And then the entire problem came tumbling out. "We were playing tag and I saw the jewelry box and the pearls were just so beautiful and they amplify magic by a factor of ten and I did touch them while Jade was still painting her nails but I didn't take them (the pearls, I mean, not Jade's nails) because I would never ever do that, but Jade's mom thinks I did and so now she won't let us hang out anymore or even do friendship mer-magic!"

Despite Brynn's crying and wailing, Will had clearly heard everything she said. That is, he understood the individual words, but he didn't completely comprehend how they all fit together. He rubbed his face again.

"Um, okay," Will stammered. "Well, listen. Uhm, don't cry. It will be okay."

"It—will—not—be okay!" Brynn groaned between new bursts of sobbing. "We—can't—be friends—anymore!"

"It'll be okay," said Will, awkwardly patting Brynn on the back, but not entirely certain if what he was saying was true. "Her mom will change her mind." Will didn't know if he properly grasped the whole story, but he was doing his best. "Or something," he added with a shrug. "Maybe you've just got to get her to see that you didn't do anything wrong—?"

"And just how am I supposed to do that?" Brynn asked. She stopped crying momentarily, a little confused about why Will was being so helpful (or trying to be helpful, anyway).

"That I don't know," said Will.

Brynn began wailing again.

Will cringed and looked around the speed-current desperately now, begging with his expression for someone to step in, to help somehow. The other passengers steadfastly ignored him. He was on his own, so he closed his eyes and took a deep breath.

"All right," he said. "Look, Brynn. I'll help ya, okay? I don't know how. But maybe I can be your replacement friend until you get Jade back. We'll figure something out. Just stop cryin', will ya?"

"I can't help it," said Brynn, sniffling and wiping her face. "I'm the saddest I've ever been. You don't know what it's like to lose your best friend."

Will looked glumly at his tailfin. "Well, that's true. I don't actually know what it's like to have a best friend in the first place."

Brynn winced. So, what Jade had said about Will was true. No friends. "It's worse for me," she said, although she wasn't one hundred percent sure about this. "I *had* a best friend and now I've lost her, and I'll never get her back! It's the worst thing in the entire world!"

"Okay, okay," said Will, rolling his eyes. "It's worse for you. Congratulations and condolences. I really do feel bad for you, honest, but bawling like a baby all the way to school isn't going to help much. If you stop crying, I'll start thinking up a plan to help you so that you can be friends with Jade again."

"*Best* friends!" Brynn corrected.

"All right, *best* friends," Will said. "Just gimme some time to think, will ya? What's missing? Jewelry? Some pearls? Magic pearls?"

"It's a string of pearls," said Brynn with a loud sniffle. "You know, a necklace. For ladies. Ten little pearls. It's very beautiful, valuable, and it's enchanted. Jade's mom is really upset, out of control."

"And she thinks you took 'em?" asked Will.

"Yes."

"But you didn't."

"No!"

"And you don't know where the necklace is."

Brynn shook her head.

William scratched his chin thoughtfully. "We'll have to find a way to convince Jade's mom that you didn't take those crazy pearls, convince her that you're not the type who would do a thing like that."

The heartbreak Brynn felt didn't go away, and Brynn was now hitching and hiccupping violently like young merfolk do after they've just finished a big crying episode, but she had to admit that Will was helping. He made it seem like there was still hope. Even if the string of pearls weren't found, maybe there was some way she could convince Mrs. Sands that she hadn't taken the necklace, or that she wasn't a bad influence on Jade.

"Thanks a lot, Will," said Brynn, sniffing and hitching.

"Think nothing of it. Are ya done with all that crying?" Will asked.

"Yeah," Brynn replied. "At least I think so."

"Good," said Will. "Now maybe I can think straight."

CHAPTER SIX

*B*rynn somehow made it through her morning classes. Then, at lunchtime, she eagerly fetched her tray and sat down at the table she ordinarily shared with Jade, hoping beyond hope that Jade would simply sit down with her and everything would be as it was before. Then Brynn waited, but she was too flustered to eat.

When she spotted Jade coming out of the lunch line, Brynn sat up straight, smiled, and gestured at the seat she'd saved. Jade made eye contact with Brynn, but shook her head sadly. Then, Jade swam to a different table and sat with some other mermaids.

Brynn's shoulders slumped, and she stared bleakly at her tuna pocket.

Will swam past with his lunch tray. "Still pouting, eh?" he asked.

Brynn glared at him. "Don't tease me, Will. Everyone is staring at me, sitting here by myself."

"I sit by myself pretty much every day," said Will with a shrug.

"Yeah, well, then you must be used to it," Brynn replied.

Will glanced around the lunchroom. "Who's staring at you?" he asked. "I don't see anyone staring at you."

"They're *all* staring at me," Brynn said. "They just quit staring when I look. Then when I don't look, they stare. I can tell. I can *feel* it."

"Well, who cares if someone's staring at you?" Will went on. "What difference does it make?"

"It's embarrassing! Don't you understand?" pleaded Brynn. "I feel like some kind of outcast or loser."

"So, sitting by yourself at lunch like I do makes you a loser?"

"That's not what I meant," mumbled Brynn, blushing.

"First of all, no one thinks you're a loser," said Will. "Everyone likes you, even though you're always getting into trouble."

"How would you know?" asked Brynn.

"I hear what people say," said Will. "I see what they do. You're very well-liked."

Brynn shrugged and poked at her lunch.

"Secondly, sitting by yourself at lunch doesn't make you a loser."

"I didn't mean to say you're a loser because you sit alone," Brynn said. "In fact, I really need to thank you for trying to help me. It's very nice of you, Will."

"That brings me to my third point," said Will. "Even if sitting alone for lunchtime did make you a loser, you're not going to be a loser because you're not going to sit alone." Will set his tray on Brynn's table and took the seat Brynn had intended for Jade. Brynn didn't say anything about her new lunchmate. She was trying hard not to be snarky to Will, but it did still feel like the other mer-kids were staring at her and judging her harshly. And besides, she did feel a little bit better having him there with her. Not that she'd ever tell him that.

"You know," said Will, "there's probably a lot of mermaids who feel like you do. If you're feeling lonely, you should look for other people who are feeling lonely, too."

"So, that's what you did?" Brynn asked with an unexpected sharpness in her voice. "You saw lonely Brynn and that's why you came over? That's why you're sitting with me?"

"Um, yeah," said Will. "Something wrong with that?"

"I wouldn't want someone to sit with me because they think I'm lonely," complained Brynn, still poking at her food but not eating it. "That's pathetic.

I want someone to sit by me because they think I'm cool or funny or nice to be around."

"Like I said, from what I hear, that's what people think. But how are you going to know who is cool and smart and funny unless you spend time with them?"

Brynn shrugged halfheartedly. He was making some good points.

"Jade's not the only mermaid in the world, you know," said Will. "There's plenty of other mermaids and merboys in the sea. Look around. There's lots of merfolk you could be friends with, some of them probably just as nice and fun as Jade."

"No way," said Brynn with a dismissive wave of her hand. "No one else is like Jade. She's my best friend. Friends like that only come around once in a lifetime."

Will stuck out his bottom lip and shrugged his shoulders up to his ears. "Maybe," he said. "I'm just saying that if you can't be friends with Jade right now because her mom won't allow it, then maybe it wouldn't hurt you to hang out with some other people."

"Like who? You?"

"Sure," said Will. "We can hang out. Thanks for asking."

Brynn lowered her eyes. It annoyed her that Will didn't seem to realize she didn't want to hang out with him. But it was possible she was even more annoyed to think that maybe she *did* want to hang out with him. Even though he didn't seem to grasp the concept of best friends, he was being helpful and kind.

"I thought you said you were going to help me," Brynn said. "I thought you were coming up with a plan for how I could be friends with Jade again. What's all this talk about making new friends and hanging out? I *have* a best friend to hang out with. Help me get her back and maybe *you* can hang out with *us*."

Will chuckled. "All right, all right," he said. "I'll keep thinking about it."

When it was time for magic class, Brynn sat in desk, assuming Jade would sit next to her, as they had arranged. Then Jade swam into the classroom, and she made eye contact with Brynn, but Jade swam to the other side of the room. Both mermaids wore very glum expressions.

First lunch, and now magic class. Brynn thought she might cry again.

Will, who was sitting behind her, leaned forward, tapped Brynn on the shoulder, and whispered, "Don't worry about it."

"Worry about what?" Brynn twisted around in her seat to face Will.

"Worry about Jade," replied Will. "I've been giving this problem a lot of thought, and I just might have a plan."

"Tell me!" Brynn insisted.

He held up a hand. "Not right now," Will whispered. "I'll tell you after school."

Mrs. Meyers swam to the front of the class. "Today is the day we are going to begin our magic amplification practice," she said, "starting with one of the easiest yet most effective mer-magical amplifiers—friendship. Everyone needs to pair up with a friend."

Brynn looked at Jade, but Jade didn't look back. Instead, Brynn saw that Chelsea, a mermaid they were both friends with, was asking Jade to be her partner. Chelsea's hair was nearly white—not as white as Jade's, but almost. Brynn suddenly felt a little hostile toward Chelsea.

What is Chelsea doing? thought Brynn, staring at the two mermaids. *Is she trying to replace me?*

Brynn didn't know it, but her face was twisted up into a scowl.

"What now?" Will asked.

"Look at those two," hissed Brynn.

"Which two?" asked Will. "This room is full of people. You're gonna have to be more specific."

"Chelsea and Jade!" Brynn snapped. "Chelsea knows that Jade and I are best friends. How dare she ask Jade to be her partner!"

"Wait," asked Will. "Aren't you friends with Chelsea?"

"Of course, I am!" whispered Brynn.

"And isn't Jade friends with Chelsea?"

"Yes! Obviously!" replied Brynn.

"Then what's the problem?" asked Will with an easygoing grin.

"You know what the problem is, William Beach! Jade is *my* best friend!"

Will shook his head. "Has it ever occurred to you that stressing out over this best friend business is causing you more trouble than it's worth?"

Brynn looked at Will sharply. "You know what, Will? I don't really see you with *any* friends. At all. So, I don't think you are an expert on friendship, okay?"

Will rolled his eyes and scoffed at Brynn, but Brynn could tell she'd hurt his feelings. She suddenly wished there was a spell for taking back unkind words. It would have come in handy right about then. But there were more pressing matters on her mind. She looked around the room, and almost everyone had found a partner. The students chatted excitedly together.

Though Brynn had been super excited to get to partner with Jade, now the assignment seemed to shine a spotlight on her lack of other close friendships.

"I don't have a partner," she said. She looked back at Will, who had slumped into his seat. "Will?" she asked flatly.

"What?"

"Will you be my partner?"

"Oh, gee, it's so nice of you to ask," he replied cheerily.

"So, you will?" said Brynn.

"I don't think so," Will answered.

Brynn put her hands on her hips. "Why not?"

"We're not friends."

"Oh, please."

"It's true," reasoned Will. "I don't have a single friend. Even you said so."

"Will you stop pouting? I'm asking you to be my partner."

"What about friends?" asked Will. "Are we friends?"

"Yes. Okay. We're friends."

"Really?"

"Yes," Brynn grumbled testily. "We're friends. Just me and you."

"You don't sound so sure."

She tilted her head. "Will."

"Okay, look," said Will. "I know you're only asking me to be your partner because you're desperate. But at the same time, I need a partner, too."

Brynn nodded. She was half-annoyed with Will but half-grateful, too.

"But could I ask you for a favor?" said Will.

"What is it?" replied Brynn.

"Just think about being friends with other

people," said Will. He shrugged. "Maybe even people like me. That's all."

"I told you," said Brynn. "We *are* friends. You and me. But I've known Jade since before I can even remember. We met when we were merbabies. She really is my best friend."

"Understood. But you can have more than one type of friend. You know that, right?"

Brynn shrugged her shoulders, but then she nodded.

"Does everyone have a partner?" Mrs. Meyers asked, raising her voice over the excited chatter of the students.

Brynn thought about Will for a moment, wondering who he'd be partners with if not her. Brynn realized all at once that something as simple as picking a partner for classwork might be a stressful and uncomfortable thing for those who don't have lots of friends or a best friend. It might even be terrifying. At first, she felt proud of herself. She had done Will a big favor by being his partner, but the more she thought about it, she realized that Will had done her a favor, too. Nobody wanted to be the one without a partner.

And so Brynn thought about how kindness was such an important thing. Kindness could transform a moment of loneliness and sadness into a moment filled with hope. This was something Brynn had never thought about before.

"Brynn?" said Mrs. Meyers. "Do you have a partner?"

"Yes, Mrs. Meyers," she replied. "It's Will!"

Will smiled shyly.

"Wonderful," she said. Then she addressed the class again. "Now, we're going to do an illumination spell, and I want you to try to cooperate with your partner and see how it increases the spell. You should be able to do much brighter and bigger spells by working together. It might be easier if you hold hands."

Will turned to Brynn and lifted one eyebrow.

Brynn was going to say, "There's no way I'm holding your hand," but Will said it first.

"We're not holding hands," he said flatly.

Brynn glared at him. Then she glanced over at Jade and saw that she and Chelsea had their hands clasped together. It really didn't seem like Jade missed Brynn all that much. In fact, Chelsea and Jade were getting along fantastically.

Mrs. Meyers said, "Let's spend the rest of the class period practicing this spell using the friendship amplifier. Remember, friendship helps make everything easier. You can do things alone, but if you have a friend, you get a better result than if the two of you did the same thing separately. Does that make sense? The result is more than the sum of its parts. If you get the hang of it, you can move on to trying other spells."

"All right," said Brynn to Will. "Let's try this."

She tried to cast an illumination spell and include Will's friendship in it. A small, fairly dim light sphere floated in the water between them.

"You did that by yourself," said Will. "You have to work with me. Teamwork, Brynn. Friendship."

They tried again, but it was no brighter than before.

Brynn heard laughter and looked over to see that the sphere of light created by Jade and Chelsea was shining so brightly, they were squinting.

"Very well done, Chelsea and Jade. You're doing great!" called Mrs. Meyers.

Brynn heard this and frowned.

"It's okay," said Will. "Don't worry about them. We'll get the hang of it."

"Maybe the problem is that we're not really friends."

"We could *become* friends, though," said Will.

Brynn wondered then what it meant to be friends with someone and even *how* to be friends with someone. If you said, "We're friends," to someone, did that make you their friend? Did you have to *try* to be a friend? Or did it just happen? She didn't even know how she and Jade had become friends. They'd known each other so long, it seemed like they had always been friends.

By the time class was over, Brynn and Will hadn't made much progress on using a friendship amplifier.

Their light spells were no brighter than they were when they cast the spell individually. This would be on the test, Brynn knew—they'd have to practice until the light they created was more than the light they could cast individually.

"We'll work on it more tomorrow," said Will. "Practice makes perfect."

"I was *hoping* I could be back with Jade tomorrow," said Brynn. "No offense, but you know. She's my bestie."

"Yeah, I get it," said Will. "But I'm pretty sure we're partners for the rest of the class. Until next semester, anyhow."

"Didn't you say you had an idea to help me?" Brynn asked, if for no other reason than to change the subject.

"I do," said Will. "But I don't want to talk about it at school. Could you meet me at the kelp forest later?"

"No," said Brynn. "I'm not allowed to hang out outside while the sea witch is still on the loose. *She's* angry at me, too, you know."

"I feel like you might be better at making enemies than friends," said Will, his voice dripping with snark.

Brynn harrumphed at him.

"If you can't go outside, that might complicate things," said Will. "Could you come to my house?

We are partners in magic class, so it won't seem too weird, right?"

"I guess that would probably be okay," said Brynn.

"Okay," answered Will. "I'll see you after school, then." He picked up his notebook and backpack, but before he swam away, he turned to Brynn and said, "Hey, I just thought of something."

"What's that?" asked Brynn.

"If Jade's not your best friend anymore, then that means I am!" He laughed sarcastically.

"Don't push your luck, William Beach."

He chuckled some more and waved at Brynn as he swam out of the classroom.

Brynn saw Jade say goodbye to Chelsea. Then Jade swam out of the room. But Chelsea didn't leave right away. Instead, she swam close to Brynn with a smirk on her face.

"So, you and Will are partners, huh?"

"Yeah," said Brynn flatly. "So?"

"So, I guess you must really like each other," Chelsea sneered.

"What do you mean?" Brynn asked.

Chelsea shrugged. "You just *really* must *like* each other."

"Not like that," said Brynn. "He's a nice merboy and we're friends."

"William and Brynn, swimming in the sea," Chelsea sang. *"K-I-S-S-I-N-G!"*

"Cut it out," said Brynn. "I thought we were friends, Chelsea."

"That was before I found out what a huge crush you have on Will. Sitting by him at lunch, and now you're his partner in magic class. I had no idea how obsessed you were with him."

Is that what everyone in school is thinking? Brynn fretted frantically. Then she shouted, "Jade is *my* best friend!"

"Mermaids?" said Mrs. Meyers from her desk at the front of the classroom. "Is there a problem over there?"

"No, Mrs. Meyers," said Chelsea sweetly. "Everything is absolutely *wonderful*."

CHAPTER SEVEN

After what Chelsea had said, Brynn wondered if it was really such a good idea to go to Will's house. However, Brynn really wanted to hear Will's idea for solving the problem with Jade and her mom and the string of pearls. She also needed lots of mer-magic practice. And so she gathered up her backpack and found her mom in the front room, reading the newspaper.

"Mom," said Brynn, "is it all right if I go to Will's house to study?"

"Will's house?" said Dana, looking up from her paper. "This is new. Are you and he friends now?"

"I guess so," mumbled Brynn.

"Golly, don't be so thrilled about it," said Brynn's mother with a laugh. "He's a nice mer-kid, isn't he?"

"Mm-hm," Brynn muttered.

"Well, are you two friends or not?" Dana asked.

Just then, Brynn's dad Adrian walked in.

"Are *who* two friends or not?" he asked.

"Brynn is friends with Will now," said Dana.

"No," said Brynn, "I'm not. I mean, I am kinda, but kinda not really."

"Then why are you going to his house to study?" asked Dana.

"Well, what I mean is, we *are* friends, but we're not *best* friends," said Brynn.

"That's okay," said Dana. "You know, you don't have to rank all your friends. Friends are friends."

Brynn thought, *That's true. But Jade really is my best friend.*

"Will. Will," said Adrian, rubbing his chin and cocking an eyebrow. "Which one's Will?"

"William Beach," said Dana.

"Oooh, yeah," said Adrian with an approving nod. "He seems like a nice mer-kid."

"Mom, Dad," said Brynn, "to tell you the truth, I'm not even sure I know what it means to *have* a friend."

Dana seemed to sense something melancholy in Brynn's response. She could often tell when something was bothering Brynn even when Brynn wouldn't clearly say so. Dana set down the newspaper and swam close to Brynn.

"Okay," said Dana. "Let's talk about that. What do you think a friend is?"

"I really don't know. I don't even know if I have any friends now that I'm not allowed to see Jade."

"Mm," said her mother, stroking Brynn's long lavender hair. "Well, what was it that made you and Jade friends?"

"We were merbabies together," said Brynn. "And you and Jade's mom let us play together a lot."

"That's true," said Dana. "So, why'd you keep on being friends when you got older?"

"Hmm. Well, we liked lots of the same things. And we had lots of fun hanging out together. Jade's always nice to me and I always try to be nice to her. We went to our first day of school together. We rode the speed-current for the first time together, and we went to our first day of middle school together. I dunno, I guess we've just always sorta 'been there' for each other."

Dana nodded. "That's great, Brynn. Sounds like you actually do know a little about what it means to be a friend and have a friend. You realize that it's more than just liking the same things. In fact, you don't even have to like the same things. Friends are people who enjoy spending time together and who treat each other with kindness. I think that's all there is to it, really."

"Yep," Brynn's dad agreed. "I think that's pretty much it."

"But I can't be friends with Will," said Brynn.

"Because if I start treating him nicely, people will say that I like him."

"You mean they'll say you have crush on him?" asked Dana.

"Yeah, exactly."

"But you don't have a crush on him?" asked Adrian.

"No," said Brynn. "And he doesn't have one on me. We just wanna be regular friends."

"I see," said Dana. "It's hard to ignore how other mer-kids feel about you, or to ignore the things they say about you at school, isn't it?"

"Yeah, it's super hard!"

"I understand. It's the same for grown-ups. But in the end, those other people don't get to decide what you do. They don't get to determine how you feel about someone. Only you can decide what your feelings are. Just because someone says something, it doesn't mean they're right. They can say whatever they want, it doesn't mean anything."

Brynn's dad listened and nodded.

"But what if they tease me?"

"That's really difficult to deal with, too, isn't it?" said Dana.

Brynn nodded emphatically.

"Well, words can be very hurtful, but they're still just words, Brynn. You know who you are, and you know your own heart. Listen to yourself. Try this:

don't react. Mer-kids usually tease each other because they want to get a reaction."

"What kind of reaction?" asked Brynn.

"Just anything, really," said Dana. "They want to embarrass you, make you upset, or make you angry. And sometimes, if you avoid giving them a reaction, they'll stop. Wanna try that?"

"So, that's how to handle bullies?"

Dana tilted her head up while she thought about this. "If it's just teasing, yes. If it goes beyond that—if someone is hurting you, it's usually time to get a grown-up involved. And you can always talk to your dad or me if anything at school is bothering you. We'll do whatever we can to help out."

"Okay," said Brynn.

"Brynn?" her mom asked. "Is someone bothering you?"

"Chelsea said that I wanted to kiss Will just because we are partners in magic class."

"And is she right?"

"No!" said Brynn.

"Then why are you listening to her? And why does it matter what she thinks?"

"I don't know," said Brynn. "It just does. She sang the K-I-S-S-I-N-G song."

"I get it," said Dana. "Just remember what I said. The only opinion that really matters is yours."

"Okay," said Brynn.

"Do you feel any better?"

"Yeah. I understand what you're saying. I just don't like it."

"And that's perfectly understandable. I don't like it either, but it'll get easier the more you practice paying attention to your own feelings instead of those of others. Focus on what you know to be true about you. That's just how it is with mer-magic: you have to tune everything else out, or otherwise, you can't cast a spell."

"Okay, Mom," said Brynn.

Dana hugged her daughter. "Now," she said. "I hope you have a productive study session with Will."

"Is it okay if I go outside if Will is with me?"

Dana pressed her lips together while she thought about this. "I don't know about that, Brynn."

"Yeah," said Brynn's dad, "we're still nervous about the sea witch."

"You said yourself that you didn't think anything would happen, and the mer-police are actively looking for Phaedra. It's been weeks and nothing has happened. Besides, Will would be with me, and he's really good at magic. And I am outside when I ride the speed-current every day anyway and—"

"All right, all right," said Dana with a smile.

"Just be careful, okay?" said Adrian.

"I will. Love you," said Brynn before heading out the door.

CHAPTER EIGHT

Brynn had never been to Will's house before, so he showed her around when she got there.

"This is the family room," said Will, "and through here is the kitchen if you want a snack or something."

They continued on through the house.

"And here's my room," he said.

Brynn looked in. There was a Jay Barracuda and the Killer Whales poster on the wall.

"Hey, I love that band," said Brynn.

"Yeah, they're great," answered Will.

On another wall, there hung a poster of the National Fishbowling League, but Brynn didn't know who any of the players were. They continued through the house.

"That's my brother's room, and there's my mom's room," said Will.

"It's just your mom's room?" asked Brynn. "Not your dad's?"

Will explained that he and his big brother lived with their mother, and their father lived in a different town. Brynn hadn't known that. But aside from that arrangement, Will's house was a lot like Brynn's. It had the same kind of glowing stones for lights, the same shell-a-vision in the living room.

"So, that's the tour," said Will.

"You have a nice house," said Brynn with a smile.

"Thanks."

Will's mom, Susan, was home, and she seemed very nice. She brought them some plankton chips to snack on. They sat munching the chips in the kitchen for a while.

Then Will asked, "So, do you want to practice the friendship amplifier?"

"Yes," said Brynn, "but, well—"

"What's wrong? What's the matter?" Will asked.

"Will," said Brynn, "I'm dying to know about the plan you thought up. You know, the plan to get Jade's mom to quit hating me."

"You don't even want to do one spell?" Will teased.

"Will!"

"Okay, okay. Let's sit down." Will directed Brynn to the couch in their living room by the shell-a-vision. "So, the problem is that Jade's mom thinks you took a necklace and because of that, she thinks you're a bad mermaid or something."

Brynn didn't like to admit it, but she had to. "Yes, but I already know that."

"Sure. Just listen. So, Jade's mom doesn't want you hanging out with Jade because she thinks your badness will rub off on her, right?"

Brynn sighed. "Yes."

Will scooted forward on the couch. "Okay. Well, what if there were something you could do that would prove you were a *good* mermaid? Something impressive and noteworthy. Maybe even something heroic."

"Okay—?"

"If Mrs. Sands could see you in a different light, she'd let Jade hang out with you again. Right? She'd almost have to."

"Yeah, but what is it that I could do?" Brynn asked.

"It'd have to be big."

"Uh-huh."

"And it'd have to be really good."

"Okay."

"And it'd have to be something that Mrs. Sands wanted."

"What is it, Will?" Brynn insisted. "Just tell me! I can't replace her necklace; it was a one-of-a-kind."

"Hang on," said Will.

He picked up the remote to the shell-a-vision and went to the menu to load a saved recording. The screen displayed the same newscast Brynn had seen with her parents that showed the arrest of the Sawfield Selkie Sisters.

"I don't understand," said Brynn.

"Don'tcha see?" exclaimed Will. "The sea witch! You helped defeat her before, right? All you have to do is figure out where she is and notify the mer-police. You'd be a hero. Even Jade's mom would have to admit it, and then she'll forget about you being a bad influence. I think there might even be a reward for information leading to her capture. Probably like a thousand sand dollars. Who knows? Maybe you really could replace the necklace."

"But I'm trying to *avoid* the sea witch," said Brynn. "I'm pretty sure she wants to turn me into a sea slug or vaporize me, and that's not something I'm really interested in."

Will shook his head. "You don't have to do anything *with* her," he said. "You don't even have to get anywhere near her. All you gotta do is figure out where she's hiding, and then call the mer-police. They'll take care of the rest."

Brynn admitted to herself that the idea wasn't terrible. She imagined herself informing the mer-police where they could pick up the sea witch. She pictured the officers swarming in and catching

Phaedra completely unaware. She'd be so angry. The mer-police would put her in handcuffs, haul her down to the mer-police station. Then Brynn imagined them throwing the sea witch in jail. Brynn would be on the Night-Sea News, on every shell-a-vision in Fulgent, standing next to the tall mer-police chief, listening and smiling for the cameras as she explained how Brynn had been "instrumental" in Phaedra's capture.

Wowee, thought Brynn. She had always wanted to be "instrumental" in something.

And finally, she pictured Mrs. Sands seeing the story, and then coming back to the Finley house to apologize for misjudging Brynn's character.

"It was all a terrible mistake," Mrs. Sands would say.

Then she and Jade would have sleepovers again, and lunches, and walks in the kelp forest, and (maybe) they could be partners in magic class again. Maybe, she thought, Will could be friends with Chelsea, and they could be partners.

"Okay," said Brynn, snapping out of her fantasy. "I like this plan. There's just one problem."

"Somehow, I knew you'd say that," said Will.

"You haven't explained how *I* am supposed to know where the sea witch is."

"I have a plan A and a plan B for that," said Will, holding up his index finger.

"What are the plans?" asked Brynn, excited beyond belief. "Tell me!"

"I'll get to that, but I want to ask a favor of you first. I really want to learn the amplifiers, and I want to pass the upcoming midterms. If you practice with me, then I'll tell you the plans, and I'll even help you carry them out."

"I feel bad that you're even asking that. I'm sorry for being so obsessed with this Jade problem. Of course, we can practice. I appreciate your help, Will. I'm not sure why you're even helping me, to be honest."

"I'd like to be friends, Brynn. And that's what friends do. They help each other out when they need it."

Brynn smiled. That's almost just what her mom had told her. Brynn was beginning to see Will in a new light.

They spent the rest of the afternoon practicing creating the illumination spell and trying to use the power of friendship to make it stronger. And it wasn't dreary or boring like some homework could be. At one point, Will's look of concentration was so intense that Brynn burst out laughing, which made Will laugh as well, and for a while, neither of them could stop, even as tears formed in their eyes.

Brynn realized she was having fun with Will. She was legitimately enjoying herself in a way she never thought she would, and this came as a bit of a shock. How had she not realized how much fun it could be to hang out with Will? Another odd thing happened: she decided she didn't care who talked or teased her about her friendship with Will.

After many attempts that resulted in only a few fizzing sparks and some sad little bubbles, Brynn and Will successfully formed a magic sphere together. Brynn smiled, and Will nodded happily. They suspended the mer-magical sphere in the water at the top of the living room cavern, and it was bright enough to illuminate the entire room.

"We did it!" Brynn exclaimed.

Susan swam into the room just as they completed the spell. "Hey, well done, you two!" said Susan. "But I'm afraid you'll have to call it a day. Will, it's dinnertime. Brynn, you're welcome to join us."

"Oh, thank you for the offer, but we're having three-shrimp salad at home tonight. My favorite!"

"I'll keep that in mind," Susan said with a laugh. "Tell your dad to give me his recipe, and maybe I'll make it for you another time."

"That'd be great!" said Brynn.

"It was awfully nice to meet you, Brynn," said Susan.

"Thanks, Ms. Beach!" said Brynn. "And you, too, Will. I had fun and we're going to get A's on the test!"

"Yep," said Will with a big grin.

Will and his mom walked Brynn to the door, and Brynn had been swimming home for almost ten minutes before she realized she'd been having so much fun, she'd forgotten to ask Will about the rest of the plan.

CHAPTER NINE

The next day at school, Brynn didn't look around for Jade. In fact, she didn't even *notice* that she didn't look for Jade. Brynn just grabbed her lunch tray, found a seat across from Will, and sat down.

"Hey, Brynn," said Will. "How's it going today?"

"It's going just fine, Will. But I left your house without asking you about the rest of the plan to locate the sea witch."

"Yeah, we had such a good time," said Will with a little snark in his voice, "we kinda forgot about the plan, huh?"

"Yeah, I guess we did," replied Brynn.

"Funny how that works," said Will. He grinned and took a big bite of macaroni and seaweed.

"Well?" said Brynn.

"Well, what?" said Will.

"The plan!" she cried. "What's the plan?"

"Oh," said Will sheepishly. "Right. The plan." He shoveled in another mouthful of lunch.

"Tell me, Will!"

"Okay," he said with his mouth still full, "but before I do, let me ask you—there's a lot of other mermaids in this school. Rather than go through all this trouble, wouldn't it be a lot easier to just find some new friends?"

"What about you?" asked Brynn. "Why don't you quit helping me and find some other friends?"

"Good point," said Will. But then he shook his head and looked down. "I'm different than other mer-kids in this school, Brynn. I never seem to fit in."

"Of course, you're different. Everyone's different, but since when is that a bad thing?"

"Trust me. I just have trouble making friends."

"Honestly, have you even tried? You're actually a lot of fun to be around, and you're nice, too. I think you are a great friend."

"Really?"

"Yeah. After I'm able to hang out with Jade again, I want you to hang out with us, too. We didn't really know you before, but Jade is going to get along with you, too. But, like you were saying, there's different types of friends. You're not going to get me interested in the National Fishbowl League, but there's probably someone out there who is. And you, me, and Jade all like Jay Barracuda and the Killer Whales!"

"You're right. I guess it wouldn't hurt to try putting myself out there and just seeing if I can make some more friends. Sure. Why not?"

"Good," said Brynn. "That's settled. Now, what is the plan?"

"Well, plan A isn't what you might call a super-clever plan, but if it doesn't work, we can fall back to plan B."

"Okay," said Brynn. "I just want to know what the plans are. Just tell me. A or B. Get on with it."

"Actually," said Will, thoughtfully tapping his lower lip with his spoon, "neither of the plans are really foolproof, but I think they're worth a try at least."

"Uh-huh," said Brynn, nodding enthusiastically. "Yes, yes. Go on."

"Plan B is more likely to work than plan A, but there are more risks involved, which is why I have it as plan B."

"Will! Tell me what the plans are! Now!"

"Okay, okay," said Will. "Plan A is just to go up to Phaedra's house by the mangrove swamp and see if she may have left any clues behind."

"That's *it*? Go to the mangrove swamp and look around? That's the whole plan? Don't you think the mer-police would have checked there already?"

"Sure, but maybe they overlooked something."

Brynn harrumphed. "Well. Okay. Tell me about plan B."

"Well, like I said, there's a lot more risks involved with plan B. I'd rather we give plan A a try first, and then we can move to plan B if it doesn't work."

"Fine," said Brynn, her attitude more than a little bit skeptical, "but you'll come with me to the mangrove swamp?"

"Of course," said Will. "We'll go this afternoon."

CHAPTER TEN

*B*rynn was still feeling a wee bit sad that she wasn't allowed to be Jade's partner in magic class, but she sure was glad to have Will as a friend as a class partner. In magic class that afternoon, while they were supposed to be practicing their friendship amplification skills, Chelsea started in again with her chant about Brynn and Will kissing in the sea. Brynn tried to pretend like she couldn't hear Chelsea, but it wasn't easy.

"Hey! Didja hear that, Brynn?" Chelsea said, clearing her throat. "Didja hear? You and Will!"

Brynn rolled her eyes furiously, but Will just shrugged it off—it was obvious Chelsea's teasing had no effect on him.

How does he do that? Brynn wondered. *How can he just* not care *what people think about him?*

Then Chelsea raised her voice. "Will and Brynn!

Swimming in the sea!" she cackled. "K-I-S-S-I-N-G!"

"Chelsea," said Mrs. Meyers sharply from her place at her desk. "Who are you kissing and why are you yelling about it?"

The other students laughed. Chelsea's face turned red, and she gave up all further taunting for the day.

"Don't get distracted, students," said Mrs. Meyers. "Keep on practicing, even if you think you're doing really well. Practice, practice, practice. I'll be back in a few minutes."

When Mrs. Myers left, Will and Brynn turned to look at Chelsea. Her face was still red, and her lips were pressed into a thin line. Will gave Chelsea and Jade a friendly wave, but only Jade waved back. Chelsea glared back.

Will and Brynn continued to practice and study. Brynn was trying to pretend Chelsea was invisible or not even in the room, but Brynn knew that Will didn't have to pretend. All Chelsea's teasing and taunting really didn't affect him, and he was conjuring up energy spheres and mer-magic spells just fine.

Maybe Mom is right, thought Brynn. *Don't react. Don't get upset. Take away the fun of it, and they'll quit. Seems to work for Will.*

"This friendship thing is really working," said Brynn, feeling happier. "Can you believe how bright this light spell is? We're gonna ace the midterm."

"Yeah," said Will with a smile. "Let's make a few

more spells. With a little more practice, we might end up casting the brightest spell in the class."

Just then, Mrs. Meyers returned to the class pushing a cart. On the cart, there was something large draped in a tarp.

"All right, class," she said, rolling the cart into the middle of the classroom. "Today, we get to learn some exciting new mer-magic—the celestial sleepiness spell."

She removed the tarp to reveal a large aquarium. Inside the aquarium, there was a small school of long, slender fish. Each was maybe the size of Brynn's forearm. Several dozens of them wriggled in the aquarium.

"These are four-winged flying fish," said Mrs. Meyers.

The students *oooo*ed and *awww*ed.

"As you may know," said Mrs. Myers, "flying fish are some of the fastest fish around. They can swim at speeds of up to thirty-five miles an hour, much faster than any of us. But not only that," Mrs. Meyers added, "as their name suggests, they can fly. Who has ever seen a flying fish fly?"

Most of the mer-kids raised their hands.

"Good. Well, as you know, if flying fish are frightened or chased by a predator," Mrs. Meyers continued, "they swim to the surface, build up their speed, and then break through into the air, where they extend their fins to use as wings. It's not exactly flying like seagulls and pelicans fly. It's more like gliding. But they can soar more than a hundred feet if the wind is right."

"Wowee," said Brynn.

Will nodded, obviously impressed.

Mrs. Myers asked, "Does anyone here think they could catch a flying fish on the loose?"

A few students raised their hands.

"How about you, Manny?" said Mrs. Meyers. "Come on up here."

She beckoned to Manuel Ballena, who had raised his hand. Most mer-kids at the school just called him Manny. He was a very athletic merboy—he was on the swim team and was known to be one of the fastest swimmers in the whole school.

Manny got up from his desk, went to the front of the class, and floated at Mrs. Meyers' side.

"Okay, Manny," said Mrs. Meyers. "I'm going to —carefully—let one of these little flying fish loose in our classroom."

A buzz of excited chatter and laughter made its way through the class.

"Settle down, everyone," said Mrs. Meyers, holding her hands up. "And, everyone, stay in your seats. Except Manny, of course. I'm gonna release one of these little fishies, and Manny's going to try to catch him. Right, Manny?"

"No problem," said Manny confidently.

More chattering and giggling and gasps erupted

from the students.

"Calm down, class. Calm down," said Mrs. Meyers. Then she slid the lid of the aquarium just slightly aside. One of the fish inside wriggled through the gap and instantly darted into the water above the heads of the seated students. They all looked up into the water, their eyes and mouths wide open.

"Get 'em, Manny!" cried Mrs. Meyers.

Manny sprang into action, rushing at the little fish, but it darted to the other side of the classroom in an eyeblink. The fish moved so fast that Manny did not even see where it had gone, and the rest of the students had to point and cry, "There it is! There it is! Over there!"

Brynn wondered how any predator could ever catch one of these quick little fish. Manny made another try to catch the flying fish, and he did better this time, keeping up with the flying fish as it swam in a tight circle around the outer perimeter of the room. The turbulence in the water sent papers, notebooks, and pencils swirling through the class. Merkids cheered and hooted and rooted for Manny to catch the fish, which frantically but rather easily left Manny in its wake. Soon, Manny was panting like a dogfish while the flying fish looked quite rested and ready to continue.

"Seems like that little fish might be a bit too fast to catch just by chasing," said Mrs. Meyers.

"Do I hafta keep chasing that little guy?" asked Manny.

"No," said Mrs. Meyers with a sympathetic smile. "I think he made his point. Well done, Manny. Take your seat."

Manny looked relieved to return to his desk. A few of the mer-kids patted him on the back and said, "Good try, Manny!"

"As you can see, these little flying fish will be the perfect test subjects for our sleep spell practice. It won't hurt them, and it will provide a challenge. You'll need quick, accurate spell-casting skills to put the fish to sleep, and friendship amplification will be just the trick to enable you to do it. Find your partners, everyone, and let's go outside!"

Out in the water of the courtyard, the afternoon sun was shining down in bars of misty light. The students gathered around Mrs. Meyers, almost unable to contain their excitement.

"There are plenty of fish in this tank," said Mrs. Meyers. "So, each pair of partners should be able to capture at least one with a sleep spell. If you're able to put one to sleep, try for another. Remember, you're in partnerships. One person in the partnership will have to cast the sleep spell on the fish, but these fish will escape fast, so use your friendship amplification to get 'em quick. Be creative and work together!"

Brynn and Will looked at each other. Both were a little nervous, but they'd been making the friendship amplifier work, so they were eager to test their skills. They watched carefully as Mrs. Meyers demonstrated how to cast the celestial sleepiness spell, and then Mrs. Meyers told the mer-students to separate into their partnerships.

"You cast the spell," said Will quietly. "I'll amplify."

"Okay," Brynn replied. "And if it doesn't work, we'll switch."

"Good idea."

"Okay, here we go," said Mrs. Meyers. "I'll count it down from five."

Brynn looked at Will, and he was already concentrating on her. She could feel the mer-magical power burst. He was doing a great job!

"Five! Four! Three! Two! One!" She flung aside the lid, and there was what seemed like a long moment before the fish realized they could swim free, but when they did, it was like a silvery sunburst. Fish swam in every direction, and the students followed.

Despite the pandemonium, Brynn singled out a fish and sped after it. The fish was too fast for Brynn to catch, but she followed it up into the water, and with Will's help, she conjured an energy sphere and shot it directly at the fish as it zigged and zipped through the water of the playground. Her first try missed, so Brynn began to conjure the spell again, but she found that she couldn't properly conjure the magic and keep the fish in view at the same time. When she aimed at the fish, the spell's power faded, and when she focused on the spell, she lost track of the fish. This was to say nothing of the fact that fish and shouting mer-kids and magic energy spheres were zipping and darting everywhere in a colorful monsoon of sparkling magic and flashing scales. Brynn saw Jade and Chelsea chasing one of the fish together, working together to corner or corral it. It wasn't working, but they appeared to be enjoying themselves.

But Brynn couldn't spot a single partnership that had actually put a fish to sleep. She looked at Mrs. Meyers—she stood near the open aquarium, chuckling as her entire class chased crazily through the playground. Brynn tried zapping another fish with her spell, but she could tell Will was losing focus, too, so she swam back to him.

"This will never work," said Brynn with a frustrated sigh. "These darn fish are just too fast."

"You're right," said Will, ducking as several fish flashed by, followed by several students. "How can we cast the celestial sleepiness spell when we can't even get close to it? Look, not a single one of us has been able to chase one down."

"Maybe that's the point," said Brynn. "Maybe we're not supposed to chase them."

"Hey, yeah," said Will, tapping his head with a finger. "I think I may have an idea."

"What is it?"

"Well," he said thoughtfully, "it might be easier to show you than tell you. Let's just stay here for a minute. You'll know pretty quick if my plan works."

"That's better than chasing one of those crazy fish all over the ocean," said Brynn.

"Focus on our friendship," said Will.

"Okay," said Brynn. She focused on their friendship, and she instantly felt the amplification working. "Are—are you going to cast a spell?"

She looked at Will. He had an energy sphere conjured, but he held onto it.

"Not yet," said Will. "Get your sleep spell ready."

Brynn conjured a magical sphere and held it between her hands. "Which fish should I cast it on?"

"None of them—yet," said Will. "Just wait."

The other students continued to dash and swirl through the water. They laughed and hollered and called out to each other. The fish zigged and zagged through the water. Brynn watched them all. They were swimming in all directions—up, right, down, left, and every other way. She was about to ask Will about this weird plan of his when, all at once, one of the flying fish whizzing past her stopped in mid-water. Well, it didn't stop completely, but it slowed down so much that it might as well have stopped!

"What in the sea?" Brynn asked herself. She looked at Will.

"Now!" he cried. "The sleep spell!"

Brynn hastily zapped the fish with the sleep spell, and the fish instantly drooped. Fish don't have eyelids, but this one was obviously very sleepy and was grabbing a mer-magical nap.

Mrs. Meyers must have been watching Will and Brynn, and she must have realized they'd taken a different approach.

As soon as the fish was asleep, she said, "Very well done, Brynn and Will!"

The other students stopped to look, and at that moment, Mrs. Meyers snapped her fingers, and the other fish returned to the aquarium, apparently under a spell Mrs. Meyers had cast on them before.

"Did you see that, class? While everyone else was busy chasing something they couldn't catch, Will and Brynn were using their heads!"

Brynn glanced at Jade and Chelsea. Jade flashed Brynn a smile and held out a thumbs-up. Chelsea scowled with envy.

"William, would you like to explain what you did?" asked Mrs. Meyers.

Will looked a little sheepish. He swam forward and said, "Well, I have this hack I've been working on. I call it my 'grab spell.' It's a reverse speed spell combined with a modified hold spell. It's like having a big pair of invisible salad tongs. I can grab something on the other side of the room and bring it to me. I use it to get the shell-a-vision remote or snacks when I don't want to get up from the couch."

"I thought so," said Mrs. Meyers. "That is a very advanced technique that you wouldn't have been taught until next year. This is what I mean by being creative with your magic. And working together. Will cast his hacked spell and Brynn put the fish to sleep —and both spells had the friendship amplifier. Great job, you two!"

Will and Brynn grinned with pride.

Mrs. Meyers continued. "But I must say, you've all done very well today—I saw many of you casting very good spells with your friendship amplification! Just do yourselves a favor and always remember: not only can friendship work to amplify mer-magic, it can also be used in an ordinary way to work together and come up with plans!"

Brynn and Will high-fived each other. For the first time since Mrs. Sands had told her she couldn't see Jade anymore, Brynn felt really happy. Will was turning out to be a really great friend, for one thing. Also, Windy Meyers was her favorite teacher. Everyone admired Mrs. Meyers for her magical skill and her kindness, and so both Will and Brynn were especially pleased to receive compliments from her.

Mrs. Meyers then let the fish out of the aquarium, and this time, all of the students were able to cast the celestial sleepiness spell on the flying fish by using various cooperative plans and tricks. Afterward, Mrs. Meyers led her class back into the school. Class was almost over, and the students got ready to go home.

Brynn was putting her notebook into her backpack when she heard a familiar voice behind her.

"Hi, Brynn."

Brynn turned around and saw Jade. She waved shyly.

"Hey, Jade," said Brynn. It was the first time they'd spoken in days and days, and it felt so good, Brynn thought she might cry. But she didn't.

"Good job with your spell," said Jade. "When Mrs. Meyers took us out to the playground, I kinda guessed it would be you and Will who'd catch the first fish."

"Aww," said Brynn, "thanks. Will and I weren't so sure."

They laughed.

Brynn added, "It was Will's plan! He's pretty smart."

"So, I guess I've been replaced by Will?" asked Jade.

"No way," said Will, startling Jade and Brynn. He'd heard them talking and had approached without their notice. "Nobody could replace you, Jade. Brynn still talks about you all the time."

Jade smiled at this. "Really?"

"Of course, *dahling*," said Brynn with a laugh. "In fact, Will is helping me with *another* plan that will allow us to be friends and hang out together again."

"What's the plan?" Jade asked, her eyes growing wide.

"Will thought that maybe if I could help the mer-police apprehend the sea witch, your mom would realize that I'm not a bad influence."

Will nodded.

"Interesting," said Jade. "Do you really think it would work?"

"What else can I do?" said Brynn, holding up her hands. "What else can anyone do? I just wish those pearls would turn up."

"Thanks for helping, Will," said Jade.

Will shrugged one shoulder. "Everyone knows you guys are best friends. It's just not right that you can't see each other."

"When all this is over with," said Brynn, "we'll all hang out. Will is really fun. And he even listens to Jay Barracuda and the Killer Whales!"

Jade sighed. "Oh, I hope the plan works!"

"I guess we'll see," said Brynn.

Just then, Chelsea swam up. "Uh, Jade," she said in a tense tone, "shouldn't we be going?"

Jade sighed again. "I better go, or *someone* might snitch on me. Good luck, Brynn. Thanks again, Will. I'll be sending good thoughts your way, and I hope it works, but most of all be careful, *daahhlings*!"

"We will!" said Brynn.

"I mean it," said Jade. "You still can't do a bubble of protection spell. I'd rather you be safe, even if it meant we could never be friends again."

Brynn knew she meant it.

CHAPTER ELEVEN

*U*nlike most trees that grow on land, mangrove trees grow in thick mud where the ocean tide rolls in. Most trees don't like salt water, but the twisted and convoluted roots of the mangrove trees filter out the salt, so they don't seem to mind salt, and they're often found growing near the ocean.

Phaedra the sea witch had used her magic long ago in the mangrove swamp to create a wondrous mansion that she called home. The mangrove roots, vines, trunks, and branches were magically grown and intricately woven into great chambers and rooms. There were corridors, arches, spires, and balconies, all constructed of delicately interlaced and braided branches, vines, and roots. The mansion seemed to hover above the water's surface. And although the surrounding area was muddy and brackish and overgrown with swampy vegetation, the mansion of the sea witch was nevertheless darkly majestic and even beautiful in its own sinister way.

The sea witch was not living there at that time, of course, and she hadn't been there since she'd escaped from the Fulgent mer-police. She was now a fugitive from justice, and no one knew where she was. Her mangrove mansion did not appear to be wholly abandoned, but it was empty and quiet and dark inside.

While Brynn loved going to the kelp forest, something about the seaside mangrove forests gave her the creeps. It was easy to get lost in the mangrove forest, for one thing, and even when Brynn wasn't lost, there always seemed to be something dreadful lurking in the dark recesses of the massive mangrove roots. She'd been skeptical of Will's plan beforehand, but now, as the two mer-kids approached the mansion of the sea witch, Brynn's nervousness about the place got worse.

"I'm not sure it's such a great idea to be here," said Brynn to Will as they swam toward the great mansion. "Her house isn't even underwater, so we can't really go in and look around, and I'm sure the mer-police searched everything here already, anyway."

"True," said Will thoughtfully. The mansion loomed above them now. "I just thought maybe we could take a look around and see if there was anything they missed or left behind. Maybe we'll find a clue."

"But Will, we're just middle-schoolers. What could we possibly figure out that the mer-police couldn't?"

"Brynn, don't say that. We're smart mer-kids! Maybe we'll see something that they saw but ignored. And aren't you practically a friend of the sea witch? You've spoken to her, been around her."

"Yeah, I spoke to her," mumbled Brynn as she eyed the mansion's towering façade, "while she was trying to blast me into smithereens."

"Well, let's just have a look," said Will, swimming up to a staircase at the grand entrance of the mansion. He lifted himself up to see the doorway. The great double doors were constructed of what looked like old passageway doors from an ancient sailing ship. "How can it hurt to just look?"

"I'm not sure, but I'm sure it might," responded Brynn, her eyes darting from shadow to shadow. "What if Phaedra comes back? What if there are magical booby traps? Look at this place. It's seriously creepy. I don't like it here at all. Why would the sea witch want to live here?"

"Maybe it's 'cause no one else does?" suggested Will. "She really seems to like being by herself. In fact, I think that's one of the reasons she is so against the humans. Phaedra wants to keep them away from her home."

"Could be," said Brynn.

The sea witch's mansion was suspended between many massive mangrove trees, above the water of the mangrove swamp, and this allowed Will and Brynn to swim beneath the water and around it. They threaded their way through the maze of roots and warped tree trunks. Now and then, they surfaced to peek into the mansion's windows and doorways.

"I wish we could see inside better," said Will, stretching up out of the water and craning his neck.

"Well, we can't," said Brynn flatly. She remained low in the water, as if hiding, ready for anything but hoping for nothing.

The two sank beneath the water and swam directly under the house. The entire structure was like some gigantic, complicated basket, and so there were small spaces and cracks to see through. The two mer-kids moved from room to room, peering inside from below or lifting themselves to see through the windows. In one room, they saw a bed and an elegant vanity mirror draped in moss. In another room, there was a reading chair and bookshelves that seemed to have grown up and out from the floor. Next, they came to something like a kitchen or maybe a laboratory, where they saw a table and what looked like a fireplace designed for cooking. Here and there stood vials and glass jars of dark liquid. Bundles of strange dried plants, flowers, and roots were suspended from the ceiling. The windows and basket-like walls allowed sunlight to filter in, but it was broken into thin, eerie rays, and there were many corners and passages that remained dark. Brynn shuddered at the thought of Phaedra appearing suddenly and catching them in the act of snooping around her house.

Looking up through the woven floor, Will said, "There's some papers on that table. Think it could be something useful?"

"I don't know, Will," said Brynn. "How long do you think we're going to stay here?"

Without answering, Will swam under the floor where he saw the papers, trying to see them. He found a skinny length of driftwood and poked it through the gaps in the basketwork of the floor, jabbing at the table and the papers on top of it. Working with his tongue sticking out of the corner of his mouth, he finally pushed the papers off the table. They fluttered to the floor. Will peeked up at them. Brynn joined him. They were glossy and colorful. Brynn saw photos of beaches and humans having fun. Will tried to wriggle his hands through a gap in the floor to retrieve the papers, but his hand was too big.

"Can you grab them?" asked Will.

Brynn's hands were a bit more slender, and they fit into the gaps between the twisted roots. She reached for the papers. "Almost got it," she grunted as she groped and gripped. Her fingers extended for the papers like the legs of a crab. At last, she got hold of a corner of one of the pages. "Got 'em!"

She pulled the papers down, and she and Will looked at them.

"I don't understand," said Will. "It's just a bunch of advertisements for humans going on vacations."

"No," said Brynn. "They're advertisements for sea cruises. See? They're all about different cruise ships."

"What's a sea cruise?" Will asked. "What's a cruise ship?"

Brynn explained. "Sometimes a bunch of humans will get on a huge ship and travel to different places around the sea. They have lots of food and music and dancing. It's a vacation on a ship."

Will nodded. "But why does Phaedra care about human cruise ships? You think maybe she wants to go on one of these cruises?"

"Why would she do that?" Brynn speculated. "She already lives by the sea. She can go anywhere in the sea she wants."

Will tapped his chin with his finger. "Maybe she's trying to start something like sea cruises for sea people? Like where we all go up on land and look around?"

Brynn wrinkled her nose and shook her head. "Sounds too normal for her. Too legal. Besides, she wants to get away from people, remember?"

"Oh, yeah," said Will.

Just then, a realization dawned on Brynn. This must have shown on her face because Will looked at her and said, "What?"

"I think I know why she has this sea cruise information," said Brynn.

"All right. Tell me."

"Remember how I told you about Phaedra and the Sawfield Selkie Sisters trying to sink a boat at Sunshine Lagoon?"

"Sure," said Will, and then the realization dawned on him, too. "She's trying to find a much bigger boat to sink," breathed Will.

"Yeah," said Brynn. "Much, much bigger. A ship with thousands of people on board."

"How could she sink a ship like that?" asked Will. "The Sawfield Selkie Sisters have been caught, so she wouldn't be able to make them crash into rocks. And these ships look gigantic. And tall. How would the people inside even hear the selkies singing? She'd need a whole choir of selkies. Phaedra might have powerful magic, but would it be enough to control something like this?" asked Will, tapping the papers with the back of his hand.

"I don't know," said Brynn. "But why else would she have all these brochures? Do you think the mer-police saw these?"

Will nodded. "On the news, they said that her home was searched. They were even able to use magic to allow officers to go inside. I'm sure they saw them."

"Does this really get us any closer to finding the sea witch?" asked Brynn. "It doesn't really tell us where she is. It only describes the boats and how many passengers they can have. There's no dates or times."

"Mm," said Will.

"These boats look really nice, though," said Brynn. "I bet families have a lot of fun on them. And, wowee, it looks like they can carry over three thousand people at once."

"It'd take way more than a couple selkies to sink a ship like that," said Will. "You'd need a ton of mermagical power to even bother a ship that big. Like a tidal wave."

"What do you mean?" Brynn asked. "The waves of the tide wouldn't affect a ship this big would they?"

"No, I mean an actual tidal wave, like one big, giant wave that collects together after large tides and winds create lots of powerful waves. If a wave is big enough, it could destroy just about anything."

"Even big ships like these?"

"Even a whole island," replied Will grimly.

Just then, Brynn thought she heard something in the mangroves—like the breaking of branches.

"Did you hear that?" said Brynn. She ducked down so that only her eyes were above the water.

"Yeah," said Will. He likewise sank down in the water.

"Is it Phaedra? Or the mer-police?" Brynn narrowed her eyes and turned this way and that.

Then she saw him. It was Ian Fletcher, the dagon. He was crouching on a mangrove root only a short distance away. Brynn gasped. Will turned to see, and he let out a startled yelp.

Like all dagons, Ian had a head like a fish and a mouthful of sharp teeth. He flashed his toothy grin at Will and Brynn. Also, like all dagons, Ian had arms and legs, almost like a human, but covered in glistening green fish scales. His hands and feet were webbed, and his fingers and toes were tipped with sharp claws. Unlike mermaids, dagons could live either on land or in water.

"Ah, little mermaid, it's you again," Ian hissed. "And a little merboy. How fun."

Ian slid into the water and swam toward Brynn and Will, who both backed away.

"But," said Ian, looking from one mer-kid to the other, "what are you doing here in the mangroves? At Phaedra's house? I didn't know merfolk came around these parts."

"We're looking for Phaedra," said Brynn.

Ian raised one of his fishy eyebrows. "And why is that?" he asked.

"She's wanted by the mer-police," said Brynn, her voice a little shaky now.

"Mm," said Ian. "I think I'll help you." He said the words in a tone of voice that made Brynn think he wanted to do anything but help them. "Yes. Why, I think I'll take you to Phaedra myself. She'll be oh-so-happy to see you, so happy to know you've been concerned about her."

With that, Ian plunged suddenly through the brackish waters of the mangrove swamp and surged toward Brynn, his arms outstretched to catch her.

CHAPTER TWELVE

*B*rynn dove to one side to avoid Ian, but his scaly hand managed to grab her tail.

"Leave her alone!" Will shouted.

Will lunged forward to tackle the dagon, but Ian slashed at Will with the long, sharp claws of his hands, and Will cowered back. But Ian had loosened his grip on Brynn, and she kicked and twisted her tail until she got away.

Brynn wished more than anything that she could cast a bubble of protection, but that was the one spell she still hadn't figured out. She'd tried and tried in magic class at school, but there was something about the spell that escaped her.

Will, on the other hand, had no problem conjuring protection bubbles, and so he had cast one around himself and now he used it to repeatedly ram into Ian while avoiding his sharp claws and teeth. Brynn was mentally cataloging all the spells she did know and could cast—the turbo speed, the celestial sleepiness spell, the illumination spells, the stun spells, the energy spheres of light. In that brief instant, she realized that she did in fact have access to a lot of spells, but how to use them to escape from Ian was something she hadn't yet learned from Mrs. Meyers. A speed spell would help Brynn get away, but then Will would be on his own with Ian. She was good at the sleep spell, but it wouldn't help if she accidentally cast it on Will instead. And so Brynn cast the brightest energy sphere she could and directed it straight into Ian Fletcher's face.

Ian squinted and scowled and tried to bat the sphere away, but it stubbornly remained, buzzing and dazzling and puzzling him. In the bright light, however, Brynn noticed something she'd overlooked before in the murk of the mangrove swamp—something polished and iridescent and gleaming in the mer-magical light, and the realization of what it was shocked her like nothing else.

Ian Fletcher was wearing Mrs. Sands' string of pearls around his scaly neck!

Casting her caution and fear aside, Brynn pumped her tail and rushed forward to grab the necklace. But Ian finally swept aside Brynn's magical light sphere, and as Brynn approached, Ian was glaring hotly back at her. And Ian would have slashed at Brynn with his talons, but just at that moment, Will caught up to her and swiftly pulled her away. He was swimming with a speed spell, and in an instant, they were out of the dagon's clutches.

Thinking quickly, Brynn amplified Will's mer-magic with her friendship, and the two put even more distance between themselves and Ian Fletcher. In two blinks of the eye, he was just a smudge in the gloomy, muddy waters of the mangrove swamp.

When their magic ran out, and when they were sure Ian hadn't attempted to follow them, Will and Brynn settled down in a cluster of giant clams. The clams were very old, and their shells were encrusted with barnacles and fuzzy with moss. The spaces between them made a perfect place to hide and watch.

"Thanks for getting us out of there," Brynn panted.

Will was breathing hard, too. He nodded at Brynn.

"But did you see the necklace?" Brynn asked when she'd caught her breath.

"Necklace?" replied Will.

"Yeah, Ian Fletcher was wearing a necklace. A string of pearls."

"Oh, yeah. So?"

"So, that's the necklace that belongs to Mrs. Sands! The one she thinks I stole! That's the string of pearls that started this whole trouble!"

"Oooh, yeah," said Will, nodding once again. "Well, I can see why she wants it back. It's fabulous."

"I know! It's absolutely gorgeous, and it's also super mer-magical! Jade said it can amplify any spell by ten times."

"Wow, that's a lot. Just think of what you could do with a simple light spell or speed spell with an amplification of ten times! But why would Ian have it?" said Will, shrugging one shoulder. "Dagons can't do magic."

"I think they can if they have a magic artifact like that. This giant clam here could do magic with an item like that. But, either way, I'd bet my last sand dollar that this has something to do with the sea witch. We know they work together. Maybe she ordered Ian to spy on Jade and me, and he saw us looking at the pearls that day. He must have snuck into their house and stolen it while they were gone."

"I wouldn't be surprised if he did it to get you in trouble," suggested Will.

Brynn groaned. "Well, if that was his plan, he did a great job. But I guess it doesn't matter—this will make Phaedra even more powerful. With an artifact to multiply her magic ten times, she might even be able to take down one of those gigantic cruise ships. We have to stop her!"

"Stop her? What can we do to stop her?" said Will, eyebrows hiked up.

"I don't know, but we've at least got to find her.

Not to get me out of hot water, but to make sure the mer-police put her in jail so she can't sink a human ship with thousands of people on board. But we still have the same problem we had before—where's Phaedra?"

Will narrowed his eyes. "I think it's time for plan B."

"Finally!" said Brynn. "Let's go home and you can tell me all about it."

They checked the wide blue ocean around them once more to make sure Ian Fletcher wasn't lurking somewhere nearby. When they were sure the coast was clear, they swam up out of the bed of giant clams.

But then Brynn stopped. "Wait a second," she said.

"Why are you stopping? What's up?" asked Will.

"Well, even though I've been really anxious to hear what all this plan B stuff is about, there's something else I want to do first. We might not need a plan B, after all."

"What is it?" Will asked.

"Come with me," Brynn said. "You'll see."

BRYNN KNOCKED ON THE SANDS' front door. Will floated by her side. After a moment, Jade's mom, Mrs. Sands, answered the door. When she saw

Brynn and Will standing there, she immediately frowned.

"Hi," squeaked Brynn.

"You?" said Mrs. Sands testily. "Brynn, what are you doing here? You know very well Jade isn't allowed to see you anymore."

"A-Actually," Brynn stuttered, "I'm not here to, well, uhm, I'm here—"

"You're here for what?" demanded Mrs. Sands. "Spit it out."

"She's here to see you, Mrs. Sands!" Will interjected. "It's about your string of pearls." Then he tried unsuccessfully to hide behind Brynn.

Mrs. Sands raised one eyebrow. "The pearls, eh? Are you finally ready to admit what you've done and take responsibility? Do you have my necklace? Where is it? Give it to me." She held out her open hand.

"No, Mrs. Sands," Brynn said with a gulp, "I didn't take your necklace, but now I know who did. The dagon Ian Fletcher has it. I saw it with my own eyes. I think he may have been spying on Jade and me the night of the sleepover. I think he saw the pearls and took them while you were away from home that night."

Mrs. Sands scoffed impatiently. "Brynn Finley, enough with the lies," she said, obviously growing angrier by the second.

"No, it's true," said Will, poking his head out

from behind Brynn. "I saw the pearls, too. And, may I add, I think they're quite beautiful."

Mrs. Sands acted as though she hadn't heard a word Will said. "You know, I really hoped you were here because you were ready to be honest, but I can see that it's just more of the same. A dagon spying in the night! Ridiculous! You really should be ashamed of yourself."

Brynn felt her cheeks burning again. "But, Mrs. Sands—"

"Not another word," said Mrs. Sands. From behind Mrs. Sands, Brynn saw Jade peek out of her bedroom. On her face was an expression of sadness and concern, but she didn't come out of her room. It was probably better that way, Brynn concluded.

"Wait," said Will. "Brynn is telling the truth!"

"Enough!" said Mrs. Sands as she moved back and closed the front door in their faces.

Brynn floated there with a stunned look. Will did the same. They stared at the door.

"I can't believe that just happened," said Will. "I can't believe she didn't believe us! Wow, Brynn. I'm so sorry."

Brynn sniffled away her tears and said, "Thanks, Will. And thanks for trying to help."

They swam away from Jade's house.

"She's never going to let me see Jade," said Brynn. "What am I going to do now?"

Will sighed. "I don't know, Brynn."

Will and Brynn heard a swish of bubbles behind them. They turned around to see Jade gliding shyly in their direction.

"Jade!" Brynn said.

The two mermaids hugged briefly.

"I can't stay," said Jade. "Obviously. But I heard what you said, and I believe you."

"But your mom doesn't," said Will. "And it seems like she never will."

"No, not unless we can prove that you were telling the truth," said Jade. "If the mer-police can find Ian with the necklace, that will prove you were being honest."

"We think he's going to give it to the sea witch," said Will.

"Even better," said Jade. "My mom knows the sea witch is bad news. If Phaedra is captured while in possession of the necklace, then my mom would have to believe that they stole it."

"She'd probably just say that I took it and gave it to the sea witch," said Brynn.

"Unless," muttered Will.

Jade and Brynn turned their faces to him, waiting for him to continue.

"Unless—" Will repeated, holding up a finger. "Unless!"

"Unless what?" cried Brynn and Jade in unison.

"Unless—Brynn is the one who leads to the sea witch's arrest! That solves all the problems—the humans are protected, your mom gets her necklace back, Brynn's reputation is restored, and everything goes back to normal!"

"Let me guess," said Brynn. "Plan B."

Will shook his head. "Plan C."

"What the heck is plan C?" Jade asked.

"Have either of you ever heard of Greenbeard?" asked Will.

"Greenbeard," said Jade, tapping her chin with her finger. "Powerful old mergician? Lived in a sunken ship? Had a green beard?"

"Yeah, that's him."

"Sure, I guess I've heard of him," said Jade.

"I thought he was just a legend, though," said Brynn. "Like Manta Claus or the Seastar Bunny."

"Well, I don't know about the others, but Green-beard wasn't a legend. He was a real merman and almost everything you've heard about him is true," said Will.

"Okay," said Jade. "So what?"

"So, have you ever heard of the Far-Finding Ring?" Will asked.

Brynn and Jade shook their heads.

"It was a ring that old Greenbeard sometimes wore," said Will. "He was obsessed with sunken pirate treasure, so he enchanted a golden ring. All he had to do was twist the ring on his finger, and it would show him the location of the treasures he was looking for."

"But we're not looking for sunken pirate treasure. We're looking for the sea witch, or at least the strand of pearls," said Brynn.

"Doesn't matter," said Will with a shake of his head. "As long as you know what you're searching for, as long as you can picture it in your mind, the ring will show it to you. Doesn't matter if it's a dead man's chest full of gold or an old library book."

"How do you know all this, Will?" Jade asked skeptically.

"My grandfather was in the Coast Guard with Greenbeard. He told me all about Greenbeard when we'd go on fishing trips. He told some great Greenbeard stories, my grandpa. One time, old Greenbeard was caught in the clutches of a giant squid with nothing but his Fish Army Knife and a bottle of rum and—"

"Will, there's no time for that!" snapped Brynn.

"Oh. Yeah. Sorry," said Will.

"And besides, this still doesn't solve our problem," added Brynn, "since we don't know where the Far-Finding Ring is."

"Oh," said Will, "but what if I said I did?"

"So, you are saying not only was Greenbeard a real merman, but he also happened to have a magic ring, and you know where to find it?"

"Yep," said Will. "My grandpa told me all about it. And he told me about this one time when Greenbeard was exploring the Craggy Deeps and—"

"Will!" cried Jade and Brynn together.

"Right, sorry," stammered Will. "I'll tell ya that one later."

"If your grandpa knew where to find the Far-Finding Ring, why didn't he go find it himself?" asked Jade.

Will shrugged. "He said he didn't need it. He's not interested in treasure."

"So, why haven't you ever gone to find it?"

Will rubbed the back of his neck. "Well, there's a difference between knowing where something is and being able to *get* it."

"What now?" asked Brynn.

"My grandpa said it's in Greenbeard's old sunken ship," said Will.

"So?" said Jade.

"An old sunken ship in shark country."

"Oh," said Brynn.

"In a sea chest."

"Oh," said Brynn. "That'll make it easier to find, I guess."

"A *locked* sea chest."

"That figures," said Brynn. "So, what are you thinking? We just swim down to some dangerous old sunken ship, past the vicious sharks, and grab it?"

"Yeah, that's the plan," said Will.

"And what do we use to unlock the chest? Birthday wishes?"

"I didn't say it would be easy," said Will.

"Yeah, well, there's easy and not easy and then there's impossible. Let's think about this. How in the world are we going to get past a bunch of sharks, find some old sea chest in a giant ship, and then somehow manage to get it unlocked?" asked Brynn.

Jade sighed. "I don't know, but I have to go back before my parents notice I'm gone." She sighed again. "Maybe we'll get lucky and the mer-police will catch the sea witch on their own."

"Yeah, maybe," said Brynn. "Hey, why don't the mer-police get the Far-Finding Ring?"

"A lot of people, especially mer-adults, don't believe it really exists," said Will. "Even my mom doesn't believe it. They think that Greenbeard and the Far-Finding Ring are just legends, too, but my grandpa told me it was all real, and I believe him. Did you ever hear the story about when Greenbeard fought off a pack of killer whales and—"

"I gotta go," said Jade. She gave Brynn a hug and she even gave one to Will. "Thanks, you two," she said glumly. "Good luck." Then she swam away.

"Don't look so discouraged," Will said to Brynn. "Where there's a will, there's a way."

"Yeah, that's a nice saying, but we're going to need more than just desire to find a way out of this."

"No," said Will. "Not *will*. Me, *Will*. Where there's a Will, there's a way."

Brynn laughed. "You're funny, William Beach."

Will grinned a big, cheesy grin, and this made

Brynn laugh some more, but under it all, she was still worried.

Why must it all be so impossible? she thought.

How could she possibly get the Far-Finding Ring to locate the sea witch and turn her into mer-authorities and save all the people on some random cruise ship, which, for all they knew, was already on its way? Not to mention the problem of being friends with Jade again. Just thinking about it made her head hurt. Still, there was something about Will that made the impossible seem almost do-able.

CHAPTER THIRTEEN

*W*hen Will came into the cafeteria at lunchtime the next day, Brynn was already sitting at their designated table. She had watched Jade and Chelsea come in—Chelsea put her nose in the air as she drifted by, but Jade had waved a sweet but nervous little hello. Brynn returned the greeting, but the two friends did not speak to one another. Then Will came in. He let his backpack settle on the floor and then set his lunch tray on the table.

"I have terrific news," he said, smiling.

"You've figured out how to get past the sharks and unlock Greenbeard's sea chest?"

"No, still working on that."

"Oh, okay. Well, gimme the good news," said Brynn.

"I said *terrific* news," corrected Will.

"Fine. Gimme the *terrific* news," replied Brynn.

"I've been thinking about what you said about trying to make friends, so I put myself out there, and I did it! I've made some new friends."

"Will, that's wonderful! And honestly, I'm not surprised. You never give yourself enough credit. You're funny and cool and you're very helpful when escaping mangroves swamps and mean dagons. I can't imagine anyone not wanting to be your friend."

Will shrugged, blushing slightly. "Yeah," said Will. "They're a great bunch of guys. We've got all kinds of plans to hang out, and do stuff, and do stuff while we hang out."

"Well, where are these awesome friends of yours?"

"Over there." Will jerked his chin in the direction of another table where a group of eighth-grade merboys was sitting.

"Whoa, eighth-graders, eh? Impressive. Why aren't you sitting with them?"

Will tipped his head to the side. "I didn't want you to be alone. I know you don't like to sit by yourself, so I thought I'd stick with you until we get this Jade problem sorted out."

"William Beach! I don't know what to say! That's so thoughtful and nice of you. You're right, I really do like having company at lunch, but I can sit by myself for a day or two. If you've got new friends, you should sit with them. Maybe we can take turns or something."

"You mean that?" asked Will.

"Yeah," said Brynn. "Go sit with them. I'll be all right."

Will raised his eyebrows. "You're positive?"

"Absolutely. Thanks for thinking of me, but I'm really happy you met some new pals. Go hang out with them, and I'll see you in magic class."

Will nodded. "Okay, I will. Thanks, Brynn."

"No problem," said Brynn.

Will snatched up his backpack, grabbed his lunch tray, and hurried over to the table with the older merboys.

From across the lunchroom, Jade saw what had happened and shot Brynn a curious glance. Jade couldn't speak to Brynn, but she and Brynn had been friends for so long, Brynn instantly knew Jade's glance meant, "Why is Will sitting over there now? Is something wrong? Are you angry at one another? What happened?"

Brynn looked back at Jade with an expression she knew Jade would interpret as, "No, no. Everything's fine. Will's just getting to know some new friends of his."

Jade gave Brynn another look that meant, "Oh, good. I was worried there for a second."

Brynn shook her head and made a face that said,

"No, it's totally cool. Thanks for checking, though. Hey, can you believe these awful clamburgers?"

Jade looked at Brynn to say, "Yeah, they're terrible. Mine's still half-frozen!"

Although Brynn really did want Will to get to know these other merboys and to make new friends, she actually felt extremely awkward sitting by herself. She decided that if Will could open himself up to new people, she could, too. She picked up her lunch tray and looked around the cafeteria. She spotted some mermaids she had met before, but didn't know very well and swam up to their table.

"Is it okay if I sit with you?" Brynn asked.

The mermaids nodded their heads and moved their belongings to make room for Brynn.

"I love your hair," said a mermaid with big hoop earrings and short orange hair.

Brynn grabbed a lock of her lavender hair and looked at it. "Really? I always thought white hair was the prettiest," she said.

The girl with the earrings shook her head so that the big hoops swayed dreamily. "I think your hair is absolutely lovely."

To Brynn's surprise, the mermaids spoke with her and asked her questions and were very friendly. It wasn't difficult at all for Brynn to picture herself being their friend and hanging out with them and shopping together and listening to Jay Barracuda and the Killer Whales. Soon, Brynn began to relax, and before she knew it, lunchtime was over.

Nevertheless, Brynn kept her eye on Will. She'd grown somewhat protective of him, and when she glanced his way, she watched in horror as one of the older merboys grabbed Will's backpack and dumped out the contents. Will's papers and books and pencils floated forlornly around the lunchroom. All of the merboys were laughing, including Will. He laughed as he scrambled to gather his things, but Brynn could tell it wasn't a genuine laugh. Then the other merboys got up from the table, and each of them gave Will a harsh shove as they swam out of the lunchroom.

Will laughed more. "Wow, what a bunch of pranksters! Thanks, guys! See you after school!"

Brynn frowned, but the bell had rung, and she had to hustle off to class.

Later that afternoon, however, when Will swam into magic class, Brynn immediately said, "Will! I saw those merboys dumping out your things and pushing you around."

"Oh, uh, that?" Will rubbed the back of his neck sheepishly. "No, yeah. They were just messing around. They're a lot of fun."

"It didn't seem like you liked it, though."

Will shrugged. "That's what friends do."

"Really?" Brynn asked.

Will frowned. "Are you jealous because I didn't have lunch with you? I knew I shouldn't have left you there."

"What? No! I actually had a nice lunch with some other mermaids who I didn't know very well. I'm just worried your new friends aren't really that nice."

"Maybe you just don't get jokes. Besides, merboys are different than mermaids."

"Okay," said Brynn. "Don't get angry, Will. I just wanted to make sure you weren't being bothered by them."

"They're my friends, Brynn. Friends. Don't you get it?"

"I suppose so," said Brynn, still somewhat suspicious. "I'm sorry. I must not have seen what I thought I saw."

"Yeah, I think you were mistaken."

The two of them stopped talking about it, but when they were practicing their magic in class that day, they weren't able to get the friendship amplifier to work for any of their spells.

"Don't worry," advised Mrs. Meyers. "Everyone has off days now and then. You two just need to get back in sync. I know you can do it. You are the four-winged flying fish sleep spell champs of class."

But Will didn't say much to Brynn for the rest of the class, and he left the room quickly when the class was over. Then, after school that day, as Brynn was headed to the speed-current stop, she saw Will again with his new, so-called friends.

"See you later, Spill," one of them said in a harsh tone.

Then two of the merboys grabbed his backpack again and began playing keep-away with it. Will tried his best to keep a smile on his face as he snatched and grabbed at the backpack, but he ended up flustered, frantically darting back and forth between the older and taller merboys.

"Careful, Spill," said another of the merboys. "We don't want you to lose all your stuff again." Then each of the merboys slapped Will on the back of the head as they passed.

Brynn swam over to Will. "Are you okay?" she asked.

Will rubbed his head where the older merboys had smacked him. "Of course I'm okay. Why do you ask?"

Brynn didn't want to embarrass Will by saying she'd seen the other merboys playing keep-away with his backpack.

Instead, she asked, "Why were they calling you Spill?"

"That? Oh, that's just my nickname. They like to take my backpack and, well, scatter my stuff all around. For fun, you know. Playfully. Strictly for fun. So, they call me Spill. As in 'we *Will Spill*' your back-pack. Get it?"

"Yeah, I guess so. And it's supposed to be funny?" Brynn asked.

"Sure it is," said Will, chuckling half-heartedly. "I can take a joke. And they sure do play a wicked game of keep-away. Probably some of the best in the whole school district."

"I don't think those merboys are really your friends."

"What do you mean?" Will protested. "They're letting me hang out with them."

"Friends shouldn't *let* you hang out with them," said Brynn. "And they aren't treating you nicely. Friends don't try to embarrass you or trick you. They don't do things to hurt you. These merboys seem more like bullies than friends. I don't think you should hang out with them."

"That's easy for you to say, isn't it?" said Will hotly. "You've always had someone in your life to be your friend—first Jade and now those other mermaids in the lunchroom. You have no idea what it is like to not have any friends. For the first time, a group has accepted me, and now you're jealous and trying to ruin it."

"That's not it at all! I am your friend. Jade is, too! That's why I don't like seeing these guys treating you badly. I meant what I said before, anyone would be lucky to call you their friend. You're smart and loyal and interesting and funny. But you don't deserve to be the butt of the jokes. I think you should maybe try to find some other friends who will not just use you to make fun of."

"Leave me alone," said Will. There was the sting of ice in his tone. Brynn watched as he swam away, and then she got on the current and rode it home all by herself.

CHAPTER FOURTEEN

*B*rynn sat on her bed that night, dangling a piece of seagrass in front of her sea turtle, Tully, who tilted his head at it and occasionally sniffed it before falling into a doze.

Brynn's dad, Adrian, poked his head into her room. He pushed his glasses up on his nose and asked, "What's happenin'?" That's what Adrian said when he was trying to be "cool."

"Nothing," said Brynn with a sigh. "Nothing is happening at all." This was true in so many ways. Brynn couldn't play with Jade, but Brynn and Will weren't speaking to each other at the moment, so they couldn't work on the plan to capture the sea witch and save all the humans, let alone get Brynn and Jade back together, which was supposed to also make Jade and Brynn and Will all good friends, but it

wouldn't because nothing at all was "happenin'."
Brynn sighed again.

Adrian swam into the room and sat beside Brynn
on her bed. "Have you and Jade been able to patch
things up?"

"No," said Brynn. "Her mom still thinks that I
took her strand of pearls, so she won't let Jade see me
or talk to me or anything."

"I'm sorry, hon. That must be really tough. Have
you been spending time with any other friends? Or
making any new friends?"

Brynn thought about the mermaids she'd sat with
at lunch, but then she thought about Will, who
maybe wasn't her friend anymore.

She sighed. "Not really."

"I see," said Adrian.

Brynn thought her dad might start in on a lecture
about talking to new people and making an effort to
make new friends, but instead, he only nodded his
head and sat there on the bed, looking like he was
deep in thought. They sat there for a while, and
Brynn was grateful for the silence.

Then she said, "Dad, why is making friends so
hard?"

Adrian looked at Brynn. Then he looked out the
window, where silvery moonlight was filtering down
through the waves. "Before I answer," he said, "let's
go for a little swim. It's a full moon tonight. Let's go
take a look."

Outside the house, the three of them—Brynn, her dad, and Tully—swam slowly through the water around their neighborhood. The moon was bright and full and cast shimmering rays of light through the dark water. They swam to the surface, and the moon beamed down, bright and cool. Its pale face was reflected on the gentle waves of the ocean.

"Wowee," said Brynn, gazing at the moon and feeling the night breeze in her hair. "It's so beautiful."

"That it is," said Adrian, nodding. "I find it interesting that all of the light from the moon is borrowed from the sun. The sun doesn't care who likes it or what is cool. It just does its own thing, shining on the Earth and on the moon and anything else around. The moon takes the light from the sun and it reflects it in our direction, and the sea reflects the light of the moon."

Brynn thought about this for a few moments, turning it over in her mind. "So, what you're saying is that I shouldn't worry about whether people like me. I should just be myself and do my own thing. And in that way, I'll shine, and others will notice and invite me into their lives? Like the moon does with the sun?"

"Hmm," said Adrian with a smile. "Maybe that's what I'm saying. But then again, maybe I was just talking about the moon."

They began swimming back home at a leisurely pace.

"Making friends can be frustrating," said Adrian. "I think that's mainly because some people won't or can't be our friends."

Brynn nodded sadly.

"On the other hand, making friends doesn't have to be so difficult," Adrian added. "If you're kind and honest and loyal, people will come into your life, and some of them will be your friends."

That's what happened with Will, Brynn thought.

He and Brynn had shown one another a little kindness, and now they were friends.

Will's new friends aren't very kind to him, though, she thought.

"Can someone be your friend, even if they aren't nice to you?" asked Brynn.

Brynn's dad thought about this as they swam along. "I think everyone has bad days, and they might say or do something they shouldn't. Even friends can make mistakes, but those days should be the exception. If so-called friends are insulting you or hurting your feelings on a regular basis, or making you do things you don't want to do, then they're not really friends."

"What are they, then?"

Adrian shrugged. "Just merpeople, I guess."

"But what if you don't have any other friends?" Brynn asked.

Adrian stopped and turned to face Brynn. "Well, don't forget to be a friend to yourself, Brynn. Let me tell you, you can be a really good friend to yourself if you try. If you're kind and honest and loyal to yourself, I think you'll find that you'll like yourself quite a bit, just like any other friend. Be supportive of yourself, spend time with yourself, and always be there for yourself."

Brynn hadn't really thought about that before—being her own friend. It sounded like a pretty good arrangement. Just then, Tully bumped Brynn with his head, as if to say he'd object if Brynn ever tried to say she didn't have any friends.

"Oh, Tully, I know you're my friend," said Brynn to the sea turtle. "And we'll always be friends. I'm talking about someone else."

Adrian swam in the direction of home with strong, slow strokes of his tailfin, so that Brynn and Tully had to hurry to keep up with him.

"I know this stuff with Jade hasn't been easy for you," said Adrian, "but just hang in there. These things tend to work themselves out. Or maybe you'll find new friends. But I promise you things will get better."

"Thanks, Dad."

The moon seemed to brighten as they swam the rest of the way home. A school of silvery smelts passed by, their scales glinting in the light. The undersea was very peaceful, and Brynn felt glad her dad had invited her to go for a swim. Despite how sad and even frightened Brynn had been without

Jade, she now felt less worried. She was still concerned about the situation with Will, however. She wondered if that was perhaps a new aspect of friendship she hadn't experienced before—standing by them even when they told you to go away. As Brynn went to sleep that night, she knew one thing for certain: she would stand by Will no matter what.

*a*t the speed-current stop the next morning, Brynn spotted Will. He wasn't acting like his confident, happy self, which made Brynn sad. She tried to swim in his direction without actually seeming to swim in his direction. She was a bit worried Will would swim away from her as she approached him, but he didn't.

"Hi, Will," she said as though nothing were wrong, as though they had not disagreed the day before.

Will perked up somewhat and said, "Hi, Brynn. Before you ask, I still haven't figured out a way to get past the sharks."

"Oh, that's okay," said Brynn. "I actually just wanted to see how you were doing."

Will nodded. "I'm good. Really good. Now that

I've got a bunch of new friends, I'm really great. It's awesome."

"That's good. It really is good to have friends."

Will didn't say anything, but he may have narrowed his eyes at Brynn.

"Hey, speaking of that," Brynn added, "I just wanted to let you know that I'm sorry if I seemed bossy or mean yesterday. As long as you're happy, then I'm happy."

"What do you mean?"

"I mean I just want you to be happy. We're friends. So, I hope you're happy."

"Why wouldn't I be happy? For the first time, I have real, actual friends. They let me sit with them at lunch. You remember how awful it was when you found out Jade couldn't sit by you anymore."

"Yeah, I remember," said Brynn. "And if you say you're happy even if they dump out your backpack or call you names, then I'll support you. But if you ever need to talk or if you need help, I'm always here for you. We're friends now."

Will swallowed heavily. "Thanks, Brynn. But I'm good. Really. Those guys just like to mess around."

Brynn nodded. "Okay, then."

They rode the speed-current to school, and when they got off the current, Will's eighth-grade friends were right by the stop, waiting for him.

"Hey, Spill!" they called. "We been waiting for ya!"

Will's hair was always stylishly combed, but one of the boys immediately messed it. Then another shoved him. And then they grabbed his backpack and started tossing it around. Will smiled and chuckled uncomfortably. At one point, he made eye contact with Brynn, and she could tell from the look in his eye that he wasn't enjoying their taunting, but Brynn wasn't sure what she could do. If she told them to stop, it might embarrass Will, and might even make him feel worse. Brynn could tell a teacher, but Will and the merboys would probably just say it was horseplay.

Brynn sighed. Maybe this was one of the hardest parts of friendship—letting your friends make choices for themselves, even when you didn't agree with them. She would just have to do what she could to support him while he made his own choices.

For the rest of the week, Will continued to sit with the eighth-graders at lunch while Brynn joined various tables, making new friends. Will's new friends persisted in calling him Spill and pushing him around, but Brynn didn't say anything more about it to Will. During magic class, she'd ask him how his day was going, and even though they weren't eating lunch together anymore, their friendship seemed to be growing stronger. In fact, on Thursday afternoon, Mrs. Meyers came and spoke to them during magic class.

"You two have got it figured out," said Mrs.

Meyers. "You are completely in sync, and it's making your amplification work perfectly! Now you can try expanding and broadening it—like casting spells farther away."

Brynn never thought she could be perfectly in sync with anyone besides Jade. She had always thought it was fate that had brought her and Jade together, but perhaps friendships were more about making an effort to help and support each other. And even though Will didn't say anything about it, Brynn suspected Will was tiring of the older merboys' harassment, so she wasn't surprised when he showed up at the lunch table she was sitting at on Friday afternoon.

"Hey," said Will. "Can you believe this? Fish sticks again."

Brynn introduced Will to the other mermaids and merboys at the table she was sitting at and then invited him to join them. They spent the lunch break talking with students who they usually didn't see much, and Will seemed to genuinely enjoy it.

As they were clearing their trays, Brynn asked Will, "How come you didn't sit with your other friends today?"

"Oh, them?" said Will. "Yeah, they're not as cool as I thought. To be honest, I'm kind of sick of them."

Brynn only smiled.

"But another reason I came to find you was

because I thought of a way to get into Greenbeard's ship," Will continued.

"I thought we'd given up on that," said Brynn.

Will shook his head. "I know you still miss Jade. She seems really nice. If we can do something to make it so Jade's mom will trust you again, I want to help you do that. Then all three of us can hang out."

Brynn smiled. They truly were friends. "Thanks, Will! So, what's the plan?"

"It's easy," said Will. "We go to Greenbeard's ship. We use the celestial sleepiness spell with a friendship amplifier to put the sharks to sleep, then we zip in, find the chest, and take the chest out of there. We can try opening it later when we're safe. Then we use the ring to locate Phaedra, we tell the mer-police, they recover the necklace, and Jade is your friend again. Bubble-bing, bubble-boom. So, what do you think?"

Brynn tilted her head. "I'm not sure. These are sharks we're talking about. Could be risky. I mean, it *is* risky."

"Oh, come on. We have gotten so good at casting spells together. Completely in sync, that's what Mrs. Meyers said. Don't you want to hang out with Jade again?"

Even after all those days, Brynn still missed Jade horribly.

"How many sharks are there?" Brynn asked.

"Probably just two or three. It'll be easy because

sharks have little brains. We can put them to sleep no problem. It would be a lot harder with a dolphin or an octopus, but sharks don't have a lot going on upstairs."

"We'll have to be really careful," said Brynn, nibbling a fish stick. "I still can't do a bubble of protection spell."

"If you need one, I'll make you one," said Will.

"And then what will you do if you need one?"

"Look," said Will. "We can just go check it out and see how it looks. How about that? If it seems dangerous at all, we'll leave and think of something else."

"Okay," said Brynn. "Are you sure you want to do this?"

"Sure I do," said Will. "I get the thrill of adventure and exploration. The sea witch gets captured, and I get to help my new friend."

Brynn smiled. "You're pretty awesome, Will."

"Thanks," he said. "You're not so bad yourself."

CHAPTER SIXTEEN

*B*ecause the sea witch was still on the loose, Brynn hadn't spent much time outdoors. She hadn't even taken Tully up to the surface lately; instead, her father, Adrian, had taken care of Tully's walks.

So, it felt weird to be going somewhere so far from home, but Brynn reasoned that she had asked her mom if she and Will could spend time outside, and her mom had told her that she could, so long as they were careful and Will was with her. Well, Brynn reasoned, Will would be with her the whole time, and the word "careful" was kind of a matter of opinion, wasn't it? It was the sea witch her parents were worried about, not sharks, and Phaedra wasn't anywhere to be seen. In fact, her parents seemed to worry less and less about Phaedra as time went by. Frankly, so had Brynn.

Why would someone so powerful be interested in me? she thought.

While Brynn did feel a bit of apprehension, it also felt really nice to be outside again. And to be outside for an adventure that would result in getting her best friend back—well, it just didn't get any better than that!

Brynn realized that being able to go outside each day and admire all the beauty the ocean had to offer was something she hadn't fully appreciated until she wasn't allowed to. It felt freeing for her and Will to be outside again, and that alone put a bit of energy into her swim strokes. She felt good. So good, in fact, she couldn't help but feel like things were going to work out, and maybe this Far-Finding Ring of Greenbeard's would be the key to it all.

Will knew where Greenbeard's old sunken ship was because his grandpa had shown it to him once, and Will was so impressed by it that he had never forgotten its location.

"Supposedly, all of Greenbeard's treasure is in that old ship," said Will.

Of course, Will and his grandpa hadn't gone into the ship, where the sea chest was supposedly stored. They'd just looked at the outside from a safe distance —knowing that sharks lived in and patrolled the surrounding area.

As they swam along, Will and Brynn talked about

their classes and their new friends and their cooperation in magic class.

"I think we're both going to do really well on our tests this semester," said Will.

"Oh, we'll get the best scores in the school!" replied Brynn.

"Careful what you say," teased Will. "Remember that bet we had?"

Brynn laughed. "Gosh, how could I forget?"

Soon, they reached a deep canyon in the seafloor. It was dark and rocky, and there were only scavenger fish around.

"It's up ahead," said Will, pointing.

As they glided over the undersea canyon, they saw it—Greenbeard's sunken ship. It was so rusted and rotted and covered with moss and seaweed, it almost didn't even look like a ship anymore. But it was massive—a very old ocean freighter with big iron smokestacks. As they swam closer, Brynn saw the old railing and chains and hatch covers.

"Wowee," breathed Brynn.

"This type of boat was built for cargo," said Will. "It's got a huge hold with room for lots of crates and shipments."

There was a gaping hole in the hull—it was presumably the damage that had caused the boat to sink.

"That hole was made by cannon fire," said Will.

"Probably sunk during one of the human wars. They're always fighting with each other."

The two of them swam down into the canyon and hid behind a rocky outcropping that overlooked the ship from high above. And while they watched, a great white shark swam slowly out from the gloom. Its tooth-filled mouth gaped, and it moved stiffly. The massive fish had small black eyes that scanned the valley with an expressionless gaze. Brynn hadn't seen a great white this close up before because the merpeople kept far away from them. They built their cities in areas where there weren't many of the big sharks around. If dangerous sharks were ever spotted near a merfolk city, shark patrols were called to gently direct them somewhere else.

Brynn was astounded at how big the shark appeared, even from such a distance. It had to be eighteen feet long—almost five times longer than Brynn. The mighty great whites ate lots of different kinds of sea life, but they *could* eat almost anything—and that definitely included mermaids and merboys. The shark lazily circled the giant sunken vessel as though it were guarding it. Soon, it was lost in the murk again. When Brynn felt herself exhale, she realized she'd been holding her breath.

Her heart was beating fast, too. She turned to Will and said, "That was a great white!"

Will nodded. "Yeah. But remember, their brains are really small. We can do the spell from here and put him fast to sleep. Don't be scared." But while Will's words sounded confident, his voice was more than a little shaky.

Just then, a second hulking shape appeared.

"Will, another shark!"

"Isn't that the same one?" Will hissed.

"No! It's even bigger than the first one!"

"Okay," said Will. "We expected this. There's probably two or three sharks hanging out here. That doesn't change anything. We've gotten good enough that we should be able to put all three of them to sleep, no problem."

Usually, sharks roamed around on their own. But sometimes, when something interesting was happening, they gathered around. And if they ever detected food, well, you get the idea. They were much more dangerous in numbers, and the higher the number, the greater the danger. Brynn only hoped she and Will could also work together to keep themselves from becoming a great white's lunch. The two mer-kids watched for more sharks.

Only one more shark came into view. But that was three of them, and it meant they were outnumbered. One shark would be challenging enough to deal with —three would be very difficult. The three sharks circled the ship like a deadly merry-go-round.

"There we go," said Will. "There's three sharks, just like I expected. I think we should go for it. We can easily do the celestial sleepiness spell from here.

Once we make sure they're good and asleep, then we sneak in, get the sea chest, and get out of there. Piece o' crab-cake!"

"I suppose," said Brynn quietly, "it wouldn't hurt to do the spell from here. We'd be able to see if they were asleep without putting ourselves in much danger. And then I guess it wouldn't be that big of a deal to just sneak into the ship real quick." But even as she spoke, Brynn felt shaky and unsure of the plan. The sharks passed by again while Will and Brynn whispered and watched.

"Yeah," said Will, "it shouldn't be a problem."

But even after agreeing to the plan, they remained in their hiding place. It seemed neither of them was ready to go ahead with it.

"All right," said Brynn. "Let's do it. But we don't go anywhere near that ship unless we are positive those sharks are asleep."

"Deal," said Will.

Brynn and Will both took a few minutes to calm and relax themselves, which allowed them to be in the best state for casting spells. This was especially important for magic beginners who needed more concentration to cast their spells. Brynn calmed herself by closing her eyes and taking deep breaths. When she inhaled, she'd think of the word "peace" and when she exhaled, she'd think of the word "calm." And then she'd think of the things in her life she was grateful for. She kept doing this until her breathing and her heart rate slowed, and her muscles felt relaxed. It was amazing that she was able to relax, even with sharks in view. It hadn't been easy to do at first, but it was something mer-students practiced every day, and with practice, it had grown easier.

"Are you ready?" Brynn asked.

Will nodded. "Yes, I feel very calm."

"Okay, here we go."

They positioned themselves side by side so the friendship amplifier could be activated. Then, they conjured their magical energy spheres. To make the spell work, they focused on the word *sleep* and tried to move the word from their minds, down their arms, and into their energy spheres.

Mrs. Meyers had said, "Imagine the word spraying from your fingertips like a fire hose. Keep your fingers straight, and wherever they point, that is where the magic will go."

Just to be extra sure the sharks would fall into a deep, long sleep, Brynn began singing a lullaby to increase the celestial sleepiness spell's power, and as soon as she started, Will joined in. They sang:

Be still and sleep, ever so deep. There's stars in the skies, so close those eyes. Sleep, sleep, sleep.

The sharks slowed down as though all three were suddenly exhausted, but they didn't stop swimming or sink to the seafloor.

"It didn't work," said Brynn. "Did it?"

"I don't know," said Will. "I don't think so. They're still swimming, and their eyes are still open."

Brynn and Will watched the sharks as they swam in slow circles around the sunken freighter. But there was something they hadn't considered.

In order to breathe, sharks must have water flowing through their gills, and to keep water moving through their gills, they must keep swimming. They can never stop. Other types of fish open and close their mouths and flare their gills to breathe, but most sharks can't do that. Will was right that the sharks' brains are tiny, but inside those tiny brains they have a sort of autopilot mechanism to allow them to rest and swim at the same time.

In other words, sharks kept swimming, even though they were asleep.

"Well, what do we do now?" said Brynn.

"Maybe it will take some time for them to fall all the way asleep," suggested Will.

And so they watched, waiting for the sharks to stop or close their eyes or come to rest on the bed of the sea. But nothing really happened. The sharks continued to swim in a slow and lazy fashion—it was hard to know if they were asleep or awake.

"If we wait too long, the spell will wear off," said Will. "We have to do something pretty soon. That ring won't find itself—although, that's an interesting philosophical question. Could the Far-Finding Ring find itself? Whoa. My mind is blown!"

"Will," snapped Brynn. "Focus!"

"Right," said Will. "Sorry. Where were we?"

"If we swim down to the ship and the sharks are awake, they'll probably eat us. If we stay here and the sharks are asleep, the spell will wear off and they'll come over to us and eat us. We need to avoid being eaten at the very least, and preferably we need to find the magic ring."

"Right," said Will. He rubbed his chin. "I've got an idea." Without waiting for Brynn to say more, Will cast a protection bubble over himself and swam out from their hiding place. One of the sharks circled in front of them, but didn't seem to notice Will at all. Will swam alongside the shark. Will shouted, "Hey!" and "Heeere, sharkie, sharkie!"

Nothing happened.

"Be careful, Will!" hissed Brynn, cowering behind the rocks.

Will got close enough to the shark to touch it, but he didn't. Instead, he pulled up close to the great white's big black eye. Staring into the eye was like staring directly at danger. He put his thumbs into his ears and stuck his tongue out.

The shark didn't react. It swam steadily and slowly onward. Will dared to bump the shark with his protection bubble. The shark kept swimming as though nothing had happened.

Will turned to give Brynn a big thumbs-up. Then he motioned for Brynn to follow, and Brynn cautiously swam out from the rocky outcropping. The shark swam off into the gloom. Soon, Brynn was swimming beside Will through the open water and toward the freighter. Before they descended to the bottom, where the wrecked ship lay in the sediment, another of the great whites swam sleepily past. Both of the mer-kids shrank back, but it continued on as if they weren't there.

"I guess sharks can sleep and swim at the same time," said Will.

"Wowee," said Brynn. She felt a shiver run up her spine as the shark swam past them, but in only a few more moments, she and Will reached the hulking wreck. They floated in the water before the great rotten hole in the hull. They peered into the darkness for a moment, and the mer-kids swam through.

"Wowee. We did it," whispered Brynn as they swam into the darkness.

"Well, let's not take too long," said Will, his eyes wide and staring into the unknown blackness of the shipwreck. "The sleep spell should last a while, but it won't last forever."

Brynn nodded.

And so they searched the sunken freighter of Greenbeard for the old sea chest in which the Far-Finding Ring was said to be hidden. The interior of the ship had been taken over by sea life. Anemones and corals encrusted the walls and floors. Lobsters and crabs scuttled here and there through the dark recesses. Some places were more like sea caves than an old human ocean vessel.

They searched the crew cabins. No sea chest. They searched the bridge and the many work compartments. No sea chest. They searched the cavernous engine room, where the great diesel-powered motors of the humans lay rusting and useless. But they did not find Greenbeard's sea chest. The ship went on forever, and inside it there lay dozens of compartments, holds, and passageways.

This is not to say they found nothing—there were many human artifacts to be found. There were tools and decaying furniture, and even some of the humans' old clothing. In the closet of a sleeping compartment, Will found an old jacket bearing the gold decorations of an officer. It was falling apart, but he tried it on, anyway.

"Ahoy there, me matey!" he cried to Brynn, saluting.

"Quit messing around and keep looking," said Brynn. "Without that ring, I'll never get to hang out with Jade!"

"Aye, aye, Cap'n!" he replied with a salute.

Soon, it grew late, and there was not enough light to see. Will and Brynn used mer-magical illumination spells, but they'd been searching for hours, and they knew they'd have to get home soon.

"We'll just have to come back another day," sighed Will.

Brynn reluctantly agreed. "Sorry for being snippy, Will. Thank you for all your help and planning."

"Ah, no problem," said Will. "I'm glad to help."

The two smiled and then swam up from the dark and brooding shipwreck and out into the dim surrounding ocean.

And into the path of an oncoming great white shark. He was wide awake, and he looked very, very hungry.

CHAPTER SEVENTEEN

*A*mong merfolk, there was a wise old saying: *It's never good to be in the company of a shark that has seen you first.* But that is exactly where Will and Brynn found themselves. One of the great white sharks they had previously put to sleep was now very awake and apparently hungry after his long nap.

The two mer-kids only just managed to dodge the huge fish, but it wheeled around and came at them for another attack. They had no choice but to dart back into the old freighter. They extinguished their magic light spells, but the shark came after them, anyway. It clanged and bashed around the passages and compartments. The rotting steel bulkheads shuddered and some of them gave way. Brynn and Will huddled, terrified, in a small room near the bridge.

There was almost no light now, and with wide eyes, they stared into the gloom.

"We're doomed," said Brynn.

"He'll get tired of hunting for us sooner or later," said Will.

Just then, the ominous black outline of the shark moved across the doorway. The shark apparently did not see or sense them, but the mer-kids shrank farther into the tiny room. Their backs were pressed against a utility closet of some sort. Will turned around and opened the closet door.

"Let's hide in here until he gives up," said Will.

They got inside and waited. They heard the shark banging around somewhere far off in another part of the ship.

"Think he's gone now?" asked Brynn.

"I'll go check," said Will. He conjured up a magic energy sphere and once again cast a protection bubble around himself. He carefully opened the closet door and swam out, first into the small room and then into the passageway beyond. Will was even bold enough to cast a light spell. He shined its beam through the passage and the bridge, but there was no sign of the great white.

When Will swam back to the utility closet, he saw a light shining within. He opened it slowly. Brynn had cast a light spell in the closet.

"Coast is clear," said Will.

"Will!" cried Brynn. "Look! Look what we were sitting on!"

There, in the bottom of the utility closet, was a metal box—what a human sailor might call a "footlocker." On the lid, words could be seen. It was faded with age and difficult to read in the weird and shifting shadows, but when Brynn brought her light sphere closer, it was clear.

THIS HERE CHEST IS THE
PROPERTY OF GREENBEARD
HANDS OFF!

"The sea chest!" cried Will.

Brynn nodded excitedly. "But it's like you said—locked!" Brynn grabbed the big padlock that was firmly fastened to the latch. She tugged on it and rattled it against the latch. The sea chest was old and battered, but the metal was heavy and solid, and the lock seemed very strong.

"Well," said Will, "the sharks are gone. So, let's just take the chest home and figure out how to open it in the safety of my backyard."

"Okay," said Brynn.

The chest wasn't light, but it wasn't exactly heavy, either.

Maybe the only thing inside is Greenbeard's magic ring, Brynn thought.

There were handles on either side, and so they

carried it between them back through the ship and out of the gaping hole on the outside.

And into the path of an oncoming great white shark.

The shark had been waiting outside the ship. With its admittedly puny brain, it must have sensed that the mer-kids would emerge again, and the fish's patience had paid off. This time, the mer-kids were holding the sea chest and could not easily leap out of the way. The shark lunged forward and its powerful jaws ferociously clamped shut. Brynn thought the shark had gotten Will, and Will thought the shark had gotten Brynn. They squealed in terror.

But the shark had actually bitten down on the sea chest, and there came a furious clanging uproar as the shark chomped and shook the metal box. His teeth scraped and rasped on the metal. Will and Brynn instinctively swam to the seafloor. The shark didn't seem to notice. It chewed and flailed at the sea chest, perhaps thinking it was some heavily armored turtle or squid. This went on for what seemed like an eternity, but when it stopped, the shark had apparently run out of patience. Twice it had waited for a morsel of supper, and twice it had been denied with only a few chipped teeth to show for it. Finally, it spat out Greenbeard's sea chest and swam testily into the depths.

Will and Brynn dared to light a little magic light.

The sea chest came drifting down and landed between them.

"Wowee," said Brynn.

"We better get home," said Will.

"I think you're right," Brynn mumbled.

The sea chest was dented and gouged from the razor-sharp teeth and powerful jaws of the great white, but it seemed to be intact. All intact except one part: the latch had been broken. When Will and Brynn lifted it up, the lock dangled uselessly, and the lid was easily lifted.

"Look!" said Will. "That crazy shark did the work for us!"

Brynn's mouth fell open. "Double wowee!"

They opened the sea chest. It was almost empty. Brynn shined her light inside the chest and saw only two things: a golden ring and a small scroll of parchment. She picked up the scroll, and Will picked up the ring. Brynn unfurled the scroll. It read:

With the Far-Finding Ring, gladness shall abound

For with a twist of this band, treasures lost shall be found

"Will!" Brynn exclaimed. "You were right. It's the Far-Finding Ring." Strangely, just like when Brynn had been dazzled by the Lostland talisman, and when she had felt compelled to put Mrs. Sands' strand of pearls around her neck, Brynn felt herself drawn to the Far-Finding Ring—and not just because it could help her to be friends with Jade again. She felt as though the ring spoke to her, telling her to put it on, and she knew it must have magical properties. Even in the dark, murky waters there at the ship, the gold ring sparkled and shined.

"You try it," said Will, passing the ring to Brynn.

"It's so beautiful," Brynn breathed. She slipped it on her finger. Amazingly, it was a perfect fit.

With the Far-Finding Ring in their possession, Brynn should have thought about making their escape, but instead, she turned her head this way and that, admiring the ring and the way it gleamed on her hand.

Will broke her trance by saying, "Look at it later, we've got to get out of here. In fact, let's test it. See if you can locate those sharks."

Brynn said, "Okay. I'll try." She twisted the band of gold around her finger a few times and then, in what she thought was a serious, mer-magical tone, Brynn said, "Where are the sharks that were surrounding this old ship?"

Immediately, the ring projected images of the sharks. Will thought it was almost like the picture of a shell-o-vision screen. A human might have been reminded of a movie projector. The images wavered and warped and floated mer-magically in the water near the ring. The sharks could be seen in deep-blue waters.

"They're way out in the open ocean," said Will. "We should be safe to swim home."

"That was close," said Brynn.

Will nodded.

"We shouldn't have done that," said Brynn.

Will nodded.

"We were almost shark food," said Brynn.

Will nodded again.

"Why aren't you saying anything?" Brynn asked.

"I'm still catching my breath," said Will.

"Oh," said Brynn.

"You should have seen your face when that shark showed up," said Brynn.

"*My* face? You looked like you'd been stung in the tail by twenty-five jellyfish!"

The two friends laughed, and after a while, they were able to calm down again.

"So, we both agree that we definitely shouldn't have gone into that ship," said Will. "But at least we have the Far-Finding Ring now. You can locate the sea witch and get everything back to normal."

"Yeah," said Brynn. "But I never want to see another shark again."

CHAPTER EIGHTEEN

*T*he two friends only just made it to their homes in time for supper. Brynn, in her house and Will in his, both tried to act casual and pretend they hadn't been off on dangerous adventures.

"What's with you?" asked Will's mother.

"What do you mean?" said Will, trying even harder to pretend that nothing unusual had happened that day.

"You're acting very *casual*," said Will's mom. "Like something weird has happened but you don't want to tell me about it."

"Oh," said Will. "That. Yes, something unusual has happened."

"What is it?" she asked, narrowing her eyes.

"Remember those friends I was hanging out with?"

"Yes," said Will's mom with a bit of suspicion in her voice. "The ones who were always 'joking around' with you?"

"Yeah, them. I decided that we weren't a good fit. I've been hanging out a lot more with Brynn Finley lately."

"Oh, that's great!" said Will's mom. "Brynn's a nice mer-kid."

When Brynn got home, she immediately went outside to play fetch with Tully, and she wasn't questioned by either of her parents. At dinner, however, Brynn's mother asked, "So nice of you to join us, Brynn. What have you been up to all day?"

"Eh, not much," Brynn answered *very* casually. "I just went to this creepy old shark-infested sunken ship to hunt for Greenbeard's magic ring."

"Hm," said Brynn's dad. "Sounds like you had quite an adventurous day."

"Yeah," said Brynn's mom. "Sounds fun! Would anyone care for more sea salad?"

The next day, Brynn and Will got together in Will's back yard. It was time to try out the Far-Finding Ring.

Brynn held her hand out in front of her and twisted the ring around her finger. Will's eyes were wide.

Brynn took a deep breath and said, "I wish to find the sea witch, Phaedra."

Once again, the ring projected an image in front

of them. This time, however, the ring showed an image of where Will and Brynn were sitting. Then, in a moment, the image began moving through the ocean. It left Will's backyard and zigged and zagged through nearby areas, passing through schools of fish, cruising along craggy valleys and sea mountains, around some bends, and then rising up out of the water to reveal Phaedra, the sea witch, standing on a rocky island with the wind blowing her hair and her arms outstretched while she looked heavenward.

"What's she doing?" Will asked.

"Look!" yelled Brynn. "She's wearing Mrs. Sands' string of pearls!"

"This is just what we need," said Will. "We can take this to the mer-police and to Jade's mom. The sea witch will be arrested, and you can be friends with Jade again."

"No, Will. This is bad. Really bad. Remember, it's enchanted and the wearer's magic is increased by ten times!"

"I forgot about that," said Will. "What do you think she's up to?"

Brynn furrowed her brow and closely examined the wobbling images the ring created.

"I know where this island is," said Brynn. "It's out by the shipping lanes. It's where the human ships pass by."

"So, she really is trying to sink one of those ocean liners with all the humans on them," said Will.

"Yes, but how?" asked Brynn.

The image projected by the ring showed Phaedra conjuring and chanting. The sea around her was rough and choppy. On the horizon, black clouds were forming. Everyone knew the sea witch had the magical ability to control the weather. Phaedra could make it rain. She could make the wind blow. She could make it hail and storm. But there were limits, even to Phaedra's magical powers.

"The weather!" cried Will. "She's going to use the pearls to enhance her weather-magic!"

"That's got to be it," said Brynn. "With the pearls, Phaedra can conjure up a storm ten times stronger than usual. That really might be enough to swamp the humans' ocean liners!"

Brynn got another idea. "I wish to find the nearest human ocean liner."

The Far-Finding Ring's projection panned away from the sea witch, floating over the water, which was growing ever stormier. Forty-foot swells were forming, and the driving wind blew spindrift spray from their peaks. As the image kept moving, Brynn and Will could see that a terrible, spinning storm was forming. Even though it was mid-day, black clouds blotted out the sun, and a dark, pounding rain fell. Brynn thought it had to be the biggest and worst storm she'd ever seen.

And then the image showed a giant cruise ship.

Brynn knew from the brochures they'd seen at the

sea witch's mansion that there could be three thousand people on the ship or even more. Little human kids, human grandmas and grandpas, even babies.

"This is bad, Will. Very bad." Brynn put her hand over her mouth.

Will only nodded.

CHAPTER NINETEEN

*E*ven in the short time that Will and Brynn watched the mer-magical image of the Far-Finding Ring, the storm boiled up and blackened and blustered. The cruise ship and sea witch were near enough to one another that both could be seen at the same time in the ring's all-finding image. And the waves from the storm and wind crested higher and higher. Fifty feet, sixty feet, and more.

Waves also crashed around the rock, where Phaedra stood with her arms and staff outstretched into the air. She chanted and sang. Through the rain and lashing wind, Brynn thought she could see Mrs. Sands' string of pearls shining and flashing with mer-magic. Phaedra's hair and dress whipped around furiously, like palm leaves in a hurricane. She smiled deliriously, and her eyes shone with frantic glee.

The cruise ship plowed heavily but unsteadily

through the heavy seas. The ship rose up over the immense sea swells and then plunged down between them. Enormous waves broke against its bow. Even if the cruise ship itself wasn't overwhelmed by the waves, the people on board must be having a horrible time, rocking and surging as they were. Brynn pictured them staggering and falling on their clumsy land-legs, spilling their delicious food, and spoiling their fine clothing. They were all probably afraid and seasick and uncomfortable.

"We've got to do something, Will," cried Brynn. "Those people could drown."

"We need to go and help them," said Will, "and we'll have to hurry."

"No," said Brynn. "We can't do it ourselves. We need to go to the mer-police."

"But what about the mer-oath?" asked Will. "*A merperson is a protector of the ocean, a guardian of the sea. Wherever living things need help, that's where we'll be.*"

"That's right," said Brynn. "We need to help them, but sometimes the best way to do that is to get someone better who can help. We're just mer-kids. We need to get some grown-up help."

Will nodded. "Okay, you're right," he said, "but in that case, we really need to hurry!"

They rushed to the nearest speed-current and went directly to the mer-police station. They swam hastily to the nearest mer-officer and explained that they had seen the sea witch, Phaedra, and that she was using magic to try to sink a cruise ship. The mer-officer was wearing a mer-police uniform, including a badge in the shape of a seastar. She had magenta-colored hair that was tied into a low bun beneath her mer-police cap.

"I'm Officer Squidly," she said. "I can help. Please, tell me where Phaedra is."

"We used a Far-Finding Ring to find her," said Brynn, holding up her hand and the ring. "Here take it." She tried to pull the ring off, but the ring was stuck! It wouldn't budge. Brynn was confused; it had slipped onto her finger so easily.

The officer shook her head. "If that's really a Far-Finding Ring, you're not going to be able to take it off until you find the thing or person you've been searching for."

"You mean it's stuck?"

"Yes, I'm afraid so," said the officer. "At least for the time being. It's part of the magic. You'll have to be the one to show us where she's at."

Brynn used the Far-Finding Ring to show the officer the general area where Phaedra was at.

"Unless I'm mistaken, that's near the Rainbow Reef area," said Officer Squidly, squinting at the image. "It's out by the shipping lanes. But that area is pretty huge. Without the Far-Finding Ring, it'll be really difficult, maybe even impossible, to find her by just going there and looking around. Is there any chance you'd come with us to narrow down her location? We'll inform your parents, of course."

Brynn nodded. "Can my friend come with me? His name is Will, and he's super smart."

Officer Squidly looked at Will, shrugged her shoulders, and said, "I guess so. Any more of your friends need to come on this adventure?"

"No," said Brynn. "Just Will. He's kind and helpful."

Will smiled proudly, but he also blushed a little.

A message was sent by dolphins to notify Brynn's and Will's parents. While Officer Squidly quickly gathered a team to go stop the sea witch, Brynn waited with Will in the lobby of the mer-police station.

"I'm scared," Brynn said to Will. "What will the sea witch do if she sees me?"

"I don't think that the mer-police would let us get in any danger," said Will.

"But Phaedra already said that she was going to get me. If I show up with the mer-police, what will she do then?"

"Hang on," said Will. He cast a bubble of protection and put it around Brynn. "There ya go. And that spell was amplified by our friendship," said Will. "So, it should be extra strong and last a long time."

"Thanks, Will."

"Sure," said Will. "What are friends for?"

A dozen or so officers filed out.

"All right, you mer-kids," said Officer Squidly. Her voice was commanding and quite inspiring. "Let's go!"

Brynn had never felt so nervous in her entire life. She was equally worried about Phaedra turning her into a sea slug as she was about the humans being hurt, even though she had never met a human. But Brynn's parents had taught her that it was important to protect all life from harm—even if you didn't get any benefit out of it personally. Her mom had said that was what the merfolk oath meant. That no matter how you felt about a group or what they could or could not do for you, you helped them if they needed help, and that included the humans.

Brynn recited the merfolk oath in her mind:

A merperson is a protector of the ocean, a guardian of the sea. Wherever living things need help, that's where we'll be.

And then she swam even harder to keep up with the mer-police. She and Will used their collective mer-magic to cast speed spells, but they kept falling behind.

"Bring up the image again," said Officer Squidly.

Brynn did, and the ring showed them where to go.

"We're going to have to give you a boost spell so you can keep up with us," said Officer Squidly.

Brynn and Will nodded gratefully. All the mer-police were able to do the most fantastic turbo spells that allowed them to swim even faster than the speed-current. Being gifted at turbo speed spells was a requirement for being on the mer-police force, and they had to pass rigorous speed tests every year in order to stay on the force and get promoted.

Officer Squidly closed her eyes, her long eyelashes resting against her cheeks. She mumbled some words, opened her eyes, looked at Brynn, and then nodded her head twice.

Brynn and Will felt the warm tingle of mer-magic surge into their tailfins.

"That should make you pretty fast," said Officer Squidly. "Since you've got the ring, we'll follow you. Let's go!"

At first, Brynn didn't feel very much faster, but as soon as she began swimming, she noticed a huge difference. She glided through the water without any resistance. Even the smallest effort propelled her far through the water.

"Wowee!" cried Brynn.

"Eleventh grade," said Officer Squidly. "That's when you really learn how to go fast."

Brynn again asked the Far-Finding Ring to find Phaedra, and the ring projected the path they should take. With the turbo boost, on top of the spell she and Will had conjured, she was swimming faster than she'd ever gone before. It was dizzying, but thrilling, too. Now it was the mer-police officers who were having trouble keeping up. First, Brynn swam outside the limits of Fulgent, and then into Great Reef, where most of the dagons lived.

Several residents and children watched out their windows as Brynn and the mer-police sped by. Next, Brynn swam around an old volcano and through a kelp forest. Fish, squids, sharks, seals, and even a few whales had to scurry out of their path. Soon, the water grew cold and dark and choppy, and Brynn and Will knew from the large waves and severe weather that they were drawing close to the sea witch and her nasty plan to get revenge on the humans.

"Let's see the image from the ring once more," said Officer Squidly as they raced along through the water.

Brynn twisted the magic ring around her small finger, and the projection shone out in front of them. The officers looked carefully, pointing and consulting with each other. Brynn looked back at Will. His eyes were wide and his mouth open, but Brynn couldn't tell if he was having the time of his life or if he was scared to death.

Officer Squidly pointed ahead. "The sea witch is just around these rocks," she shouted.

"We can take it from here," Officer Squidly told Brynn. "You two go hide behind those breakers."

She and the other officers made a plan for how they would approach the sea witch, dove into the water, and swam away.

"Do you think we'll be safe staying this close?" Brynn asked.

"I don't see why not. The sea witch has got to be a long way from here. Officer Squidly wouldn't have had us hide behind the rocks if she thought we'd be in any danger."

"Our turbo spells are still active," Brynn reasoned, "so we can just take off fast if there's trouble."

"Yeah, that's true," said Will.

"Okay, let's go," said Brynn, pointing to the rocks at the surface, where the waves were crashing. "No one will even notice us." Then she added, "Probably not, anyway."

She bit her lip. The waves and wind filled the air with excitement as she and Will swam to the rocks and positioned themselves in a spot where they could see the sea witch and the cruise ship off in the distance.

CHAPTER TWENTY

ill and Brynn watched the image projected by Greenbeard's magic ring. There was Phaedra, standing tall and majestic on the rocky beach of a small island. Brynn wondered how she could hold her staff in the air for so long without exhausting herself. But Phaedra never seemed to tire, piling magic upon magic, using her powers and Mrs. Sands' enchanted pearls to summon the most terrifying storm Brynn had ever seen. The ocean swelled in monstrous black waves, rising up, cresting, and then crashing down with a great howling roar. Thunder boomed overhead, and lightning flashed. The great cruise ship bucked and tilted wildly. Brynn and Will huddled in the protection of the breakers.

Somewhere out of Brynn and Will's view, the mer-police were speeding along under the sea to stop Phaedra. Soon, they surfaced near the rocky beach.

"Look!" said Will, raising his voice over the noise of the storm. "It's the mer-police!"

The mer-police were using their turbo spells to propel them so they could then jump high out of the water like dolphins. As each one leaped into the air, they fired their spells at Phaedra.

"I think they're casting stun and sleep spells at Phaedra!" cried Brynn.

Will nodded.

In truth, the battle was so far away, and the view was so obscured by rain and fog, they couldn't clearly see what was going on, even in the image projected by the Far-Finding Ring. But they saw the magical sparking and flashing. Phaedra's storm was so intense, even the experienced mer-police officers were having trouble conjuring and aiming their spells. Over the roar of the wind and deafening thunder, Brynn was sure she could hear Phaedra cackling.

The cruise ship was rising and falling abruptly in ways that looked like it could snap in half.

Down by the island, Officer Squidly and her mer-police team were taking a beating. Phaedra seemed to be enjoying herself, pulling down and directing the sheets of rain and wind and bolts of lightning. Every time one of the mer-police officers got close to Phaedra, she held out a hand or pointed her staff, and ever more ferocious winds or devastating lightning bolts would toss the officers back. They couldn't come anywhere near Phaedra, and their spells were batted aside like helpless birds. Brynn was sure she could hear Phaedra laughing as she beat the mer-police officers back again and again.

And still, the storm strengthened. The ship rocked and plunged through the waves. Phaedra's storm seemed to encircle the huge vessel, turning it around and around like a child's toy boat. Brynn wrung her hands and bit her lips. It wasn't looking like the mer-police would be able to stop Phaedra, and worse, it seemed certain that the cruise ship might sink and take all of its human passengers with it.

After all that had happened, Brynn just couldn't believe the sea witch was going to succeed. It felt so wrong and so unfair. She was going to get away with everything. She'd escaped from the mer-police, sent Ian Fletcher to steal the enchanted string of pearls, then tracked the mighty cruise ship, and now her plan was almost complete.

All at once, Brynn had a realization. Through the roaring confusion, she realized she'd left out one critical piece of information when she'd led the mer-police to Phaedra.

"Will!" she yelled. "The necklace! The necklace of pearls!"

"What?" Will yelled back. "The pearls?"

"Yes! The pearls!"

"What about 'em?" shouted Will with a shrug.

"The mer-police don't know she has them! They

don't know about the stolen pearls, and they don't know that's why Phaedra's so powerful right now!"

"Okay," hollered Will. "So?"

"So," Brynn shouted through cupped hands, "if they knew that, maybe they could get the pearls away from her and reduce her magical power. And then maybe they could stop her!"

"So, what you're saying," cried Will, "is that we've got to find some way of letting them know."

Brynn nodded, but her expression was full of doubt and worry.

"That's what I thought," said Will. "Okay, let's do it."

The storm and sea were too loud to allow them to shout the information to the mer-police officers, and so they didn't even try. They'd have to get closer, even though that would bring them closer to the brutal storm and lightning, and also directly in the sea witch's view. It would be dangerous. Brynn was still in the bubble of protection Will had created for her, but since Brynn still couldn't do the spell, they only had one bubble, leaving Will unprotected.

"Let's try to swim closer," Will said, then added, "Carefully."

Brynn nodded again in agreement.

They dove into the churning, roiling sea and were immediately tossed around like driftwood.

"Will," Brynn yelled. "You should take the bubble

of protection. It's your spell. You should be the one to have it."

"I'll be okay," Will answered back. "If the sea witch sees us, it's you who she'll target."

That's for sure, thought Brynn.

They began swimming to where the mer-police were scattered and struggling in the water. Their turbo speeds helped them cover the distance quickly, but each time Brynn or Will tried to get close enough to get the attention of one of the officers, the wind or waves pushed them off course.

"Her necklace," Brynn shouted as loudly as she could. "Her necklace is giving her a boost of ten times more power!"

The two mer-kids tried swimming closer and hollering, but were thrown back by a sixty-foot wave. Brynn felt like a butterfly in a hurricane. Then, somehow, Officer Squidly spotted Brynn and Will. She swam over to the mer-kids.

"What are you doing?" she yelled a bit angrily. "You need to get away from here! It's no place for mer-kids! Go home now!"

"You need to take away that necklace she's wearing!" Brynn shouted.

"What?" yelled Officer Squidly. "What's she wearing?"

"That necklace!" shouted Will, trying to point at his own neck and at the sea witch simultaneously. "Get it away from her!"

A giant crashing wave broke over Officer Squidly and the mer-kids, and they were sent pinwheeling through the black water. When they recovered, Will and Brynn began to shout at Officer Squidly again, but she only waved them off.

"Go home!" she yelled. "Tell me later!" And then she sped away to launch another attack at the sea witch. And once again, Officer Squidly leaped into the air, launched a stun spell, and watched helplessly as it was deflected by the vicious wind and weather.

"It's no use," Brynn shouted to Will. "There's just no way they can hear us."

"Hey, Brynn," hollered Will.

"What?" replied Brynn.

"I got another plan!"

"Okay," said Brynn. "What is it?"

"Well," Will said thoughtfully, "it might be easier to show you than tell you."

CHAPTER TWENTY-ONE

*T*his mission wasn't going well at all for Officer Squidly and her team. She knew Phaedra the sea witch was said to have very powerful magical abilities, and she knew that Phaedra had tried to sink human sea vessels in the past. However, this storm was just outrageous, unlike anything Officer Squidly had ever seen. She almost couldn't believe Phaedra had summoned the raging storm. How could she? Squidly had seen mergicians summon storms before. But this storm was five times—no, *ten* times—bigger than any Squidly had ever seen or even heard about. The giant waves, the howling wind, the hammering rain were all too powerful to believe. But still, they had to apprehend the sea witch and save the foundering ship.

A bolt of lightning impacted the water like a bomb not far from Squidly. It was accompanied by a shattering boom, and Squidly was forced to fall back, dive beneath the waves, and steady herself for another try.

Squidly had chosen her best officers for this mission, too—Officer O'Shawnisea, Officer McScales, and Officer Welker. All three were smart, strong, and fast. And they were some of the best mer-gicians around. But no matter how they tried, it seemed like the weather and waves were always against the officers. It couldn't be just Phaedra's magic. There had to be something else at work here.

And those two mer-kids distracting us didn't help, either, Squidly thought.

It was great that the mer-kids had come forward to help the mer-police find Phaedra, and they'd led Squidly and her team straight to Phaedra. That was great. But the sea waves had risen ten feet in the time it'd taken her to send them home. What had they been trying to tell her? Something about Phaedra's neck? Squidly didn't know, couldn't understand them. Sure, they were probably trying to offer more help, but they didn't understand what it was like to take on a dangerous figure like the sea witch, especially with weather conditions like this.

And the storm just seems to be getting bigger and bigger! thought Squidly. *How is that possible?*

Squidly and her officers had regrouped and were ready to launch another attack on the sea witch.

"O'Shawnisea!" barked Squidly. "You go up the right side with rapid-fire stun spells!"

"You got it, Chief!" said O'Shawnisea. She was a strong mermaid with solid magic skills. Her hair was in a frightful tangle, and she was beginning to look tired, but she was ready for action.

"McScales! You go up the left side with holding spells! See if you can pin that sea witch down!"

"Aye, aye, Chief!" McScales was a big bulky merman with a gigantic tail and a flowing beard.

"Welker! You and I will go up the middle with a friendship-amplified turbo boost and twin stunners set on full power!"

"Let's do it, Chief!" cried Welker. She was a slender mermaid and had no big muscles, but she was quicker than a four-winged flying fish, and her magic ability was outstanding.

"On my signal," shouted Squidly, raising her arm.

She checked her officers one more time—each had their spells ready to go, and each one looked determined.

"*Now!*" shouted Squidly with a wave of her arm.

The four mer-police officers charged forward, pumping their mighty tails and riding magical speed spells and protection bubbles. Not even a killer whale could have withstood such an onslaught. There were mer-magical energy spheres and stun rays buzzing through the water and over the waves in Phaedra's direction as the officers pressed their attack. Anyone watching would assume the sea witch would be instantly overwhelmed by this show of courage and mer-magic.

But they were thrown back once again.

First, a giant surge of dark seawater, like a reverse tidal wave, threw them back, even farther back into the sea than where they'd started. Then, a brilliant volley of lightning bolts struck all around them, stunning, blinding, and disorienting them. Squidly tried to call out new orders, but the fearsome wind snatched away her commands before they could be heard.

When the mer-police officers gathered together again, they looked exhausted and worried. Squidly led them down to the seafloor for a huddle.

"What are we gonna do now, Chief?" said Welker, breathing hard. "That sea witch is unstoppable!"

"Yeah, and this weather is really kicking our tails!" O'Shawnisea complained.

"How in the ocean is she doing this?" cried McScales. "How's she generating so much power?"

"I don't know," said Squidly. "But we've got to keep trying. This Phaedra is seriously dangerous. And we've got to protect all those people on that cruise ship! Now let's go back up there and take another look at the situation."

As they swam up from the ocean floor, worn out but willing to try again, they heard someone or something approaching from behind. And whatever it was, it was swimming so fast, it was making a rushing noise the officers could hear over the sound of the pounding surf above. They turned to look.

"The mer-kids!" cried Squidly.

Sure enough, it was the two middle-grade mer-kids. They were obviously still under the influence of the mer-police's super-turbo speed spells, but they must have been using their own speed magic, too, with some awesome friendship amps. The one in the lead, the young mermaid, was inside what looked like a very sturdy protection bubble, and the one behind her, the merboy, was flapping his tail like a dolphin on a sugar-kick. All four of the mer-police officers gaped as the two mer-kids sailed by at a tremendous speed.

As they zoomed past the amazed officers, the mermaid named Brynn smiled nervously and saluted. In an instant, they were out of sight and halfway to the sea witch.

"Ah, fishguts!" said Welker. "Those mer-kids are gonna land themselves in hot water with the sea witch, and then we'll have yet another problem to solve!"

"No," said Squidly. "Follow them!"

They all put on turbo speed and started swimming their fastest.

"Why are we following them?" said McScales, swimming hard to keep up with his fellow officers.

"Because they're not going to be a problem,"

Squidly shouted back at McScales. "Those two little squirts have got a plan!"

A COUPLE OF MINUTES PREVIOUSLY, Brynn and Will were holding hands and focusing like never before on their friendship. They re-cast their own speed spells, and Will strengthened Brynn's protection bubble.

"Do you understand the plan?" said Will, still holding Brynn's hand.

"I understand the part you've told me about, which isn't very much," said Brynn.

"We're going to swim like mad straight for Phaedra," said Will. "You'll be in the lead, and I'll be pushing you from behind. With the protection bubble, you should go really fast through the water."

"Okay, I understand that part, but what happens when we get to Phaedra?" asked Brynn.

"When we get to Phaedra, I'm going to launch you right at her like a cannonball!" said Will.

"Then what?" asked Brynn.

"No more talk!" cried Will. "You just aim yourself at the sea witch. I'll take care of the rest!"

And so they started swimming. As soon as they flicked their tails, however, they were propelled forward through the water with astonishing speed. Brynn felt her whole body buzz with magic.

"What's happening?" shouted Brynn as they roared through the water like supercharged sea lions.

"It's the friendship!" cried Will. "It's really working!"

"Woooweee!" squealed Brynn.

It might have been luck or even an accident, but with the combination of the mer-police speed boost and the power of the friendship of Will and Brynn, they might have created the most powerful turbo speed spell in all mer-history.

Up ahead, Will and Brynn saw Chief Squidly and the other mer-police officers. They appeared to be huddling together, planning their next move. Brynn and Will were approaching fast.

"Watch out!" shouted Brynn. "It's the officers!"

They changed their course slightly so they wouldn't collide with the confused-looking mer-police.

As they passed by Chief Squidly, Brynn flashed them a self-conscious smile, and then, just to show they were trying to be helpful, she gave them a salute. But then they raced past, and the mer-police were out of sight behind them.

Now Will and Brynn broke through the water and surfed along the crashing waves, faster than any human speedboat.

"We're going too fast!" cried Brynn. "We're going to crash!"

"Don't worry," replied Will, his voice raised. "This protection bubble is like solid rock!"

With that, Will launched Brynn into the air, just like a cannonball, as he'd said. Brynn screamed as the protection ball began to spin and turn like a baseball in flight. But even as she turned over in the air, Brynn knew she was on a course to strike the sea witch dead center. She waited for the impact.

Brynn didn't know this, but the mer-police were following only a short distance behind. They had seen Will launch Brynn with tremendous speed. They had seen her arc through the air on a collision course with Phaedra. They held their breath and waited for the impact, too.

But at the very last second, the sea witch spied Brynn, pointed her staff at her, and shot out a bolt of magic electricity that sent Brynn flying in the opposite direction.

Just then, everything was quiet. The storm lifted. The rain and thunder and lightning were no more. The great waves calmed.

And a rainbow appeared.

CHAPTER TWENTY-TWO

*B*rynn blinked her blue eyes and stared at the sky. She was floating on her back on the calm surface of the ocean. The black roiling clouds were breaking up, rolling back, and the bright sky was shining through. Her lavender hair was spread in a sort of fan all around her in the water. A gentle sea breeze caressed Brynn's cheek. Everything was calm. There was no more thunder or wind. So, Brynn lay there for a moment, trying to figure out what had happened. From somewhere far away, she heard the call of seagulls. Everything was still.

Then she heard voices. Brynn sat up in the water and looked toward the island. There, she saw the mer-police officers and Phaedra the sea witch. She swam toward them, though now at a decidedly slower pace—her speed spells had been exhausted at last. As Brynn drew closer, she saw that Phaedra was trying to evade the mer-police—again. She fired bolts of lightning at them. She fired energy spheres to stun them. Unfortunately for Phaedra, her magic had weakened. And she was now no match for the four mer-police officers. As Brynn reached the beach, she noticed Mrs. Sands' string of pearls was missing from Phaedra's neck.

So that's it! Brynn concluded. *That's why the storm died. That's why Phaedra can't fight off the mer-police anymore. She lost the necklace.*

But how did she lose it? Brynn tried to recollect what had happened. She remembered the incredible mer-magical speed boost she and Will had conjured up. She remembered whizzing past the mer-police officers at an amazing speed. And then she remembered flying through the air on an impact course with Phaedra.

That's it, thought Brynn. *The necklace must have been knocked off when I slammed into her with my rock-hard bubble of protection!*

But she hadn't slammed into Phaedra.

No, Phaedra had used a blast of wind to toss Brynn back into the sea. Who had managed to get the string of pearls off Phaedra?

"I got it!" said a voice from somewhere down the beach. "Brynn, I got the necklace!"

Brynn turned to see Will swimming toward her along the shore.

"You took the necklace?" asked Brynn with amazement.

"Yep," said Will proudly. "While Phaedra was distracted by you and the mer-police officers, I used my grab spell to yank it off her neck!"

"Wow. Wee. Will, you did it!"

"*We* did it," he corrected. "Without all our friend-ship amplification, none of it would have worked."

They laughed and exchanged a hug, then a high-five, and then an up-high tail-slap.

"Looks like Officer Squidly's happy," said Brynn.

Phaedra was sitting elegantly on a rock. The officers had placed a hold spell on her, but Phaedra didn't allow herself to look defeated or even bothered.

"Phaedra," said Officer Squidly, "you are under arrest for the crime of attempting to inflict harm on a living being." From her utility belt, she pulled out a pair of enchanted handcuffs and placed them on the sea witch—just to be sure, Brynn thought.

The dark clouds had almost completely vanished. The sun shone warmly, and the colossal rainbow stood brightly in the sky, arcing from one horizon to the other.

"Brynn!" someone shouted.

Brynn turned to see her mom and dad splashing toward her. They instantly wrapped her in a big hug.

"I'm okay," said Brynn. "They've arrested Phaedra."

Her mother sighed. "That's a relief. Now things can finally get back to normal."

"Yeah," said Will. "Now you can be friends with Jade again."

Brynn thought she detected the slightest hint of sadness in Will's voice.

"Will," said Brynn. "You mean *we* can be friends with Jade. Best friends."

Will grinned. "*Best* friends? But you can only have *one* best friend. You even said so."

Brynn slowly shook her head. "I was wrong about that. I don't think 'best friend' means a friend who is better than all your other friends. I think it means being the best friend you can be. I've known Jade since we were wee merbabies, and she really is my best friend. I've only known you since last semester, Will, but you are a best friend, too."

Will raised an eyebrow and tilted his head. "Does this mean we have to call each other '*dahling!*' all the time from now on?"

Brynn folded her arms. "Is that going to be a problem, William Beach?"

Will laughed. "No, I guess it's not a problem, *daaahliiing!*"

CHAPTER TWENTY-THREE

*I*t had turned into a beautiful day on the ocean. The cruise ship sailed along peacefully, and the merfolk saw humans emerge from their cabins to stand on the deck of the ship. Brynn imagined they were relieved to have survived the storm and to be on stable footing. The humans were so busy looking at the rainbow and taking pictures of it, they didn't even notice the merpeople in the water below them.

It wasn't long until the entire area was buzzing with activity. The SCI—Sea Criminal Investigation— team showed up to process the scene and collect evidence. Then, reporters from the local shell-a-vision stations arrived. All of them wanted to talk to Brynn, Will, and Officer Squidly. Reporters from several stations surrounded the trio with video cameras and lights on the ocean floor.

"How were you able to locate the sea witch?" a reporter with mint-colored hair asked, directing her microphone toward Brynn.

"Will's grandpa had told him about this Far-Finding Ring, and we just asked it to help us find her," said Brynn. She held up her hand to show the ring, and then thought to take it off. She tried to slip it off her finger, and to her amazement, it came right off! Feeling relieved, she held the ring in front of the reporters so they could zoom in on it.

"Why was Phaedra's magic so powerful? How was she able to create such a terrifying storm?" asked a reporter in a deep voice.

Officer Squidly spoke up. "We believe that the suspect was wearing an enchanted pearl necklace that had been stolen from a community member. The necklace's enchantment strengthened her powers. When the necklace was removed, she returned to her ordinary abilities, allowing our officers to use their own magical abilities to stop her."

"And how did you two get involved?" said the reporter to the mer-kids. "How were two young merpeople able to help mer-police stop a powerful sea witch?"

"Well," said Will, "we're best friends."

That's when Officer Squidly said, "These two mer-kids were *instrumental* in the apprehension of the sea witch. They are to be congratulated."

Brynn beamed.

After the reporters finished asking all their questions, and everyone was packing up their things, Brynn hesitated as her parents began swimming home.

"Hey, wait!" said Brynn. "What about the string of pearls?"

"Oh," said Will sheepishly. He rubbed the back of his neck. "About the pearls."

"What? What?" cried Brynn.

"Well, when I grabbed them with my grab spell," said Will, "I guess the string broke and the pearls went flying in every direction. They're lost."

Brynn's mouth fell open, and a shocked expression came onto her face. She began to cry.

"Sorry, Brynn," said Will gloomily.

Brynn shook her head. "It's not your fault. We had to get that necklace off of Phaedra. The string was sure to break no matter what. And the wind and waves surely scattered them from here to Atlantis."

"Uhm, excuse me, *dahlings*," said Brynn's dad. "I think you're forgetting something."

Will and Brynn looked at Adrian. He was pointing at his finger, trying to give them a hint about something.

"The ring!" said the mer-kids together.

Using the Far-Finding Ring, Brynn and Will found all ten of the pearls.

"Do you think we can fix it?" Brynn asked her parents.

"We can sure try," said Dana.

Back at home, Will, Brynn, and her parents strung the pearls on a length of strong string, but something weird kept happening. The mer-magical pearls kept pushing away from each other, like magnets turned the wrong way. They tried everything. Brynn's parents tried their magic, and they all tried friendship amplification. But it was no use.

"Sorry, Brynn," said her mother. "But I think that because the necklace was originally created under special circumstances, there's not much we can do to make it like it was again."

"I just feel bad for Mrs. Sands," said Brynn.

The others nodded sadly.

The next day, Brynn swam to the Sands' home and softly knocked on the door. Mrs. Sands answered.

"Brynn!" she said. "We've just been watching you and your friend on the news! I'm so proud of you. It's very special to have someone from our very own neighborhood involved with such a great act of sea guardianship!"

Bryan shrugged and blushed.

"Come in," said Mrs. Sands. "I have some things I want to say."

Brynn swallowed, swam inside, and took a seat on the couch. Mrs. Sands sat beside her.

Mrs. Sands took a deep breath and said, "I'm so sorry I ever suspected you had taken my string of pearls. The sea witch has been after it for years. If I'd only thought about it, I would have realized who really must have taken it."

"Wowee," replied Brynn. "That's a big relief, Mrs. Sands."

"I hope this won't affect your friendship with Jade," Mrs. Sands added. "You are everything I could want in a friend for my daughter."

"Even though I haven't been able to see her," said Brynn, "Jade's still my best friend. Nothing can change that!"

"Let me go get her for you," said Mrs. Sands. She stood.

"Wait," said Brynn. "I have something for you." She handed Mrs. Sands a small satchel made of woven seagrass. Mrs. Sands poured the contents into her hand, revealing the ten pearls.

"We tried to fix it," said Brynn. "But the pearls wouldn't go back together."

"No," said Mrs. Sands. "I wouldn't think so. It was a special, one-of-a-kind necklace, and the way it was made can't be done again."

"I'm so sorry, Mrs. Sands!"

"Thanks, Brynn, but it's not your fault. In fact, you and Will are the only ones who figured out what really happened to these pearls. But you know what? This gives me a wonderful idea."

"What's that?" Brynn asked.

"You'll see," said Mrs. Sands with a smile.

"I have something else for you, too," said Brynn. She held up the Far-Finding Ring and it sparkled in front of them. She handed it to Mrs. Sands.

"To make up for the necklace," said Brynn. "And to help you in case anything else of value ever goes missing."

"I wish I'd had this back when the necklace first went missing," said Mrs. Sands. "It would have saved a lot of hurt and bad feelings. I feel so badly for having treated you that way. Will you forgive me?"

"Of course," said Brynn.

"And thank you for the ring. This will come in handy. I'm always losing my shell-phone."

Mrs. Sands let Jade know Brynn was there, and the two friends began talking to each other, filling each other in on everything that had happened in the last few weeks. Brynn was filled with so much joy, she thought she might explode. Jade was back in her life again, which made everything seem perfect.

Later that night, Mrs. Sands came to the Finley house. She apologized to Brynn's mom for her earlier treatment and then explained that she had something for her and Brynn. Brynn and her mother sat side by side while Mrs. Sands pulled out two small boxes from her purse. She gave them the boxes, and the mother and daughter opened their boxes at the same time.

Inside were beautiful necklaces, each with a single pearl.

"Instead of having one necklace that could increase mer-magic by ten times, why not have ten necklaces that could increase mer-magic by one full degree for all my friends," said Mrs. Sands.

In addition to Brynn and Dana, Mrs. Sands also gave necklaces to Jade; Windy Meyers, the magic teacher; Officer Squidly; Will's mother, Susan; and a few of her friends at the hospital.

"And the last one is for me," said Mrs. Sands.

She smiled as she rose to leave. Brynn's mom stood to walk her to the door.

"Seeing just one pearl will remind me that all the other pearls are with people who I consider to be my friends," said Mrs. Sands. "And as you know, mer-magic is much more powerful when it's shared with friends."

CHAPTER TWENTY-FOUR

*A*fter such an exciting weekend, it was hard to wake up and go to school on Monday morning, but when Brynn swam to the speed-current stop and saw Jade waiting for her like she had before all this trouble, Brynn completed three full flips.

"Wahoo!" yelled Brynn. "Jade is here! And she's my best friend!"

The mermaids gave each other a quick hug before getting onto the speed-current. Once on their way to school, Brynn spotted Will. He began swimming toward her, but a mocking voice cut through the water.

"Hey, Spill, are you going to go see your girl-friend now?"

It was one of the eighth-grade boys. Brynn instantly felt her blood begin to boil. Will hesitated, but then he kept swimming toward them.

"Aren't you going to say anything to them?" Jade asked.

"I don't owe them any explanations," said Will. "Just because they say something, doesn't mean it's true. I'm not going to waste my life trying to argue with them," said Will. Then he turned to Brynn. "I just came over to say hi. I like your necklace."

"Thanks!" said Brynn. "It was nice of Mrs. Sands to give it to me."

Will looked uncomfortably from Jade to Brynn. "Well, I guess you're friends again, so I'll just go." He began swimming away, but Brynn grabbed his arm.

"Hold up, Will!" said Brynn. "You're a best friend now, too!"

"Yeah," said Jade. "I'm really impressed with you, William Beach. I think we're all going to be best friends!"

The three of them joked and talked for the rest of the speed-current ride, and they all agreed to eat lunch together.

But when lunchtime came, Will was having a hard time getting to their table. Students, and even some teachers, kept stopping him. They'd seen him on the news and wanted to ask him all kinds of questions.

"Did you really stop the sea witch?"

"How did you do it?"

"What's she like?"

"Tell us the stories about Greenbeard."

It was almost like Will was suddenly a movie sea-lebrity. Every table wanted him to sit with them, but Will finally made it over to Jade and Brynn.

"Mermaids," said Will, "would you mind if I sit at a different table today? I've met this new mer-kid today. His name's Reggie. He had all these questions about Greenbeard. He can't get enough of all my stories! And then I found out that we have the same favorite fishbowling players, and I'd love to talk to him more about it. Would you be okay if I sat with Reggie today?"

"Of course, *dahling,*" said Brynn. "I already said that it's good to have many friends."

Will laughed and nodded. "He does seem like he could be a good friend. He's at least someone good to talk with about the National Fishbowling League."

"I'm glad *someone* likes to talk about it," Jade said, laughing.

"Okay, I'll see you in magic class," said Will, dashing off to sit with his new friend.

"I feel bad that Will is going to have to get a new magic partner," said Jade.

"What do you mean?" Brynn asked.

"Well, now that we're friends again, I just assumed we'd be magic partners now. And I'm glad. Chelsea isn't the best at partner spells."

"Actually, Jade, I don't think we should switch partners. Will helped me when no one else would.

You are my best friend, but Will is too, and I think maybe we should stick with the same partners."

Brynn was worried that this would hurt Jade's feelings or make her angry. She was worried that almost as quickly as their friendship had been restored, it would be broken again.

But Jade nodded thoughtfully. "Yeah, you're right," she said. "It seems better that way. Even best friends don't have to do *everything* together. Like you said, it's good to have multiple friends."

"Thanks for understanding," said Brynn.

"Of course, *dahling*!" said Jade, now returning to her very most dramatic-actor voice. "If I learned anything about this, it's that friendships are a wonderful and valuable thing. As valuable as—" Jade paused as she tried to think of the word.

"—as a magical string of pearls?" Brynn asked.

"Oh, absolutely," said Jade. The mermaids laughed.

As Brynn went to bed that night, Tully curled up next to her.

"Everything is back to normal now that Jade can be my friend again," she told the sleepy sea turtle. But then Brynn thought about how she'd gotten to know Will better and had made a new best friend.

Tully seemed to smile contentedly, and then he laid his head on the bed and closed his eyes.

"Actually," Brynn said quietly, reconsidering, "things are even better now."

Don't forget to download your free activity kit at
www.subscribepage.com/amandaluzzader.

PLEASE LEAVE A REVIEW

Please take a moment to review A Mermaid In Middle Grade on Amazon as this helps other readers to find the story. Thank you!

Amazon.com/review/create-review?
&asin=B0891QFGMP

In print and ebooks

A Mermaid in Middle Grade

Book 3: Voices of Harmony (releasing fall 2020)

Book 4: The Deep Sea Scroll (releasing fall 2020)

Book 5: The Golden Trident (releasing winter 2020)

Book 6: The Great Old One (releasing winter 2020)

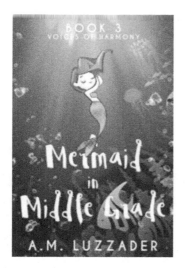
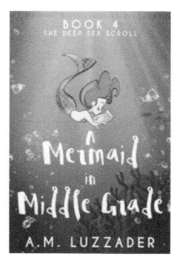

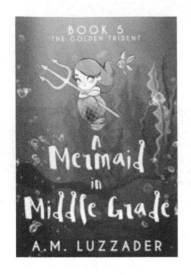

BOOK 5
THE GOLDEN TRIDENT

A Mermaid in Middle Grade

A.M. LUZZADER

BOOK 6
THE GREAT OLD ONE

A Mermaid in Middle Grade

A.M. LUZZADER

ABOUT THE AUTHOR

A.M. Luzzader writes middle-grade books for children and science fiction books for adults. She is a self-described 'fraidy cat. Things she will run away from include (but are not limited to): mice, snakes, spiders, bits of string and litter that resemble spiders, most members of the insect kingdom, and (most especially) bats. Bats are the worst. But A.M. is first and primarily a mother to two energetic and intelligent sons, and this role inspires and informs her writing.

A.M.'s favorite things include cats, strawberries, and summer. She was named Writer of the Year for 2019 by the League of Utah Writers. A.M. invites readers to visit her website at www.amandaluzzader.com and her Facebook page www.-facebook.com/authoramandaluzzader.

Visit www.subscribepage.com/amandaluzzader to sign up to receive an occasional newsletter with information about promotions and new releases. From this site you'll also be able to download a **Free Activity Kit for A Mermaid in Middle Grade.**